Romance Unbound Publishing

The Cowboy Poet

Serving his Master series Book 2

Claire Thompson

Edited by Donna Fisk

Fine line edit by Gabriella Wolek

Cover Art by Mayhem Cover Creations

ISBN 978-1456325695

Copyright 2018 Claire Thompson
All rights reserved

Chapter 1

Flames leapt through the air in flashing arcs of bronze, white and blue, looping in intricate patterns against the dark night sky. Though Tyler was drawn to the showy pageantry of the fire whip demonstration, his mind continued to linger over the words of the cowboy poet who had been on the stage a moment before.

Clint Darrow had spoken in a raspy, deep voice, his slow easy drawl stroking his words like a hand on a horse's silky mane. Tyler felt as if the cowboy had been speaking directly to him, honing in on secrets he'd buried and tried his best to forget.

The cowboy poetry and music festival was taking place both indoors and out. Inside the large western bar, a complete sound system had been erected for the musicians. Outside, behind the building, poets trooped up to recite their particular brand of cowboy wisdom on a raised stage lit by twinkling Christmas lights wound through the slats of the fencing that surrounded the courtyard on three sides. The audience enjoyed the show from picnic tables set in rows in front of the stage.

Only three months on the job, Tyler had been excited to finally get the opportunity to go out and cover his first story rather than being stuck in the office, fact checking and line-editing someone else's work. When Tyler had been assigned by *Lone Star Monthly* to cover the event, he had expected corny recitations by has-been or would-be cowboys and the same tired old country music standards offered in a nasal twang. Still, it was an opportunity to get his own byline and he had jumped at the chance to prove himself.

He'd been pleasantly surprised by the quality of the poetry and the diversity of the music, but until this particular cowboy had appeared on the scene, Tyler had been calmly wearing his reporter hat, watching from a mental distance as he sipped his beer and framed the outline of his article in his mind.

There was scattered applause and whoops as the man onstage doused his whips and offered an ironic tip of his Stetson to the crowd. "That's it for the poetry, folks," the man announced. "Stay and enjoy the music. And thanks to all the great performers tonight."

Tyler was distracted when he saw Clint Darrow moving from the side of the stage where he'd apparently been standing during the fire display. As he walked past the picnic table where Tyler was sitting, Tyler noticed he had a slight limp.

Tyler rose before he knew what he was doing, as if by some silent command. Before he could stop himself, he extended his hand. "Tyler Sutton, *Lone Star Monthly*."

The cowboy stopped, pushing his hat back as he shook Tyler's offered hand. He had a long, beaked nose and high prominent cheekbones. The man's eyes were such a dark brown that Tyler couldn't distinguish the pupil from the iris. He wasn't precisely handsome, but there was a brooding power in his face that caught and held Tyler's attention. His hands were large and calloused, his grip firm. When their eyes met, something rippled through Tyler, moving with a strange heat to the pit of his stomach.

"Clint Darrow. Pleased to meet ya."

"Damn," Tyler breathed, the word out of his mouth before he could stop it. He had heard that attraction can strike like a stray line of lightning, laying a man flat, but until that moment he had never experienced it.

Clint Darrow released his grip, stepping back. Tyler was glad for the cover of near darkness as he felt the blood move over his features like a slap in the face. He was cursed with the Sutton fair complexion and even a tan couldn't hide the dull red that would work its way from his collar to the middle of his ears. It was usually brought on by anger, but at this moment it was fueled by a rush of pure lust.

"Pardon?" Clint asked with a quizzical smile.

To cover his embarrassment at having spoken aloud, Tyler hurriedly offered, "I enjoyed your poetry very much. I'm writing an article for *Lone Star Monthly*. I'd like to interview you for my story, if you're of a mind. How about I buy you a beer?"

"That'd be right nice." Clint's smile broadened. For one crazy moment Tyler had an impulse to drop to his knees and press his face against the sexy bulge in the cowboy's jeans, right there in front of a host of God-fearing country boys, many of whom would probably like nothing better than to beat his brains out if he so much as hinted at his sexual orientation, much less offered such blatant proof.

Then several people surrounded them, including the man who had just wielded the burning whips onstage. Tyler backed to the edge of the group, watching as several men thumped Clint on the back and a woman with bright yellow hair held out the festival program, asking Clint to autograph it for her.

Clint looked past them, catching Tyler's eye. "Still want that beer?" Tyler asked, over the hubbub. Clint nodded gratefully and offered a small, rueful smile that made Tyler think he didn't really enjoy being the center of all that attention.

Tyler turned away, heading inside toward the bar. He returned a few minutes later, two cold bottles of beer in hand, scanning the courtyard for the sexy cowboy. He saw him sitting at the picnic table Tyler had recently vacated, and moved toward him. The man with the whips sat directly across from Clint.

"Mind if I join you?" Tyler focused on Clint as he held out the bottle, his stomach twisting as if he were fourteen instead of thirty. There was just enough space at the end of the bench beside Clint, who nodded and patted the wood in invitation.

Tyler tried to ignore the jolt of electric current that sidled its way through his loins when their thighs touched. He reminded himself he was on the magazine's time. He wasn't on the prowl at a pickup bar. He edged slightly away from Clint, hoping to regain his composure while he thought about how to get the interview started.

To his confused surprise, Clint shifted as well, so that their thighs remained pressed together from knee to hip. Tyler dared to glance at the cowboy, who was watching him with fathomless dark eyes, a faint smile quirking the corner of his mouth.

"You ain't from around here. I'd remember," Clint observed softly, leaving Tyler to wonder if there was any hidden meaning in his words. His hat was tipped back now, revealing dark wavy hair shot through with threads of silver. Tyler pegged him to be in his late thirties or early forties. His eyes caught and held Tyler, as if Clint were somehow speaking to him in a secret, whispered tongue only the two of them could hear.

Tyler lifted his beer bottle and drank while he tried to collect himself. He was keenly aware of the man's thigh hard against his own. He thought about shifting away again, but there was nowhere to go on the narrow bench. Besides, he didn't want to move. In fact it took all his self-control not to inch closer.

"You gonna introduce me to your buddy, Clint?" The man across the table waved his beer bottle in their direction.

"This here's Tyler Sutton. He's a reporter. Wants to interview me for a magazine." Clint grinned, revealing white square teeth against his tan face, his eyes crinkling at the corners. "And this fella," Clint nodded toward the man across from him, "is William Huckabee, or Huck to his friends. If he had any friends, that is."

With a good-natured guffaw, Huck extended his hand across the table and Tyler shook it.

"That was quite an impressive fire display," Tyler offered.

"I learned from the master." Huck nodded toward Clint. "Clint taught me everything I know about fire play. It's a real crowd pleaser. When you light them Kevlar whips with the white gas and make 'em curl through the air like snakes outta hell, folks'll get real quiet and pay attention."

"So, there's more to the poet than meets the eye." Tyler looked at Clint, impressed. He tried his best to ignore the sudden rush of blood to his cock.

"There usually is," Clint said quietly. "The longer I'm alive, the more I realize never to assume you know everything about a person. Even folks you thought you knew. Even…" he paused, those dark eyes ensnaring Tyler once again, "…yourself."

"Take Clint here," Huck said. "More to this dude than meets the eye." He offered an exaggerated wink and a sly leer in Tyler's direction. "Better watch yourself around this one, young fella'."

"What the gentleman, and I use the term loosely," Clint offered a weary but indulgent smile, "is trying to say is, watch your ass, because he labors under the fool idea that if a person is gay, they automatically lust after any guy they see, even if he's dumb as dirt and as good lookin' as the back side of a muddy hog, like my good friend Huck here."

Huck grinned, his eyes cutting back toward Tyler. "You'll have to forgive Clint, here. That's a five cent head under that ten dollar Stetson. He wouldn't know good lookin' if he fell over it." The pudgy man puffed out his chest, adding, "I'm quite popular with the ladies. Especially when they find out Clint ain't interested."

Both men laughed.

Gay.

Tyler struggled to keep his composure, wondering if the two of them were having some kind of joke at his expense. Was this guy really openly gay, right here in the middle of West Texas cowboy country? And this Huck guy, whom he'd pegged as a gun toting, dyed in the wool, rightwing reactionary homophobe, for no reason other than his birth and culture, seemed to be pretty relaxed about it as well.

Though Tyler didn't deny his own orientation, at least not since he'd moved to Austin, neither did he offer it up to strangers. It was nobody's business but his own. Yet he couldn't deny the floodgate that had opened on his attraction to Clint Darrow, the cowboy poet who talked about taming wild spirits and was at home with whips and fire. What would it be like to feel the hard press of his naked body, to taste the musky heat of his cock…

Flustered, Tyler retreated to the safety of his beer bottle, lifting it for a long drink, only to discover it was empty. He stood abruptly, praying his face and the bulge at his crotch weren't giving him away. "I'm going to get myself another beer. Can I get either of you gentleman another?"

Huck shook his head, but Clint nodded his assent. When Tyler returned with the fresh bottles, two other men had joined them, settling beside Huck. "…was the damnedest thing," one of them was saying. "One of our bull semen tanks just disappeared. Luckily it was empty, though the tanks themselves don't come cheap. But I hear over at Blake's ranch they had a couple of canisters go missing too."

Clint's attention was on the man who was speaking. Tyler did his best to ignore the lurch in his gut when their fingers brushed against each other as Clint accepted the second bottle with a distracted nod. He reminded himself to focus. He had a job to do, an interview to procure, and then, if he knew what was good for him, he'd get the hell out of there before he made a damn fool of himself.

"That's what I'm saying," the man beside Huck continued earnestly. "We lost a tank last week. I heard from Lucky Harding that they found some tanks missing too. He was fit to be tied."

Tyler, who always had an ear for a story, perked up, glad for the distraction. "Have y'all reported these thefts to the local sheriff?"

The men all turned to stare at Tyler, who was suddenly embarrassed for having stuck his nose into their business. He was again aware of Clint's thigh touching his own on the narrow bench.

"This here's Tyler Sutton, a reporter for *Lone Star Monthly*," Clint said to the two new men. Introductions were made and Tyler's shoulder brushed Clint's as he extended his hand across the table. Clint made no effort to move away. Tyler, forcing himself to focus, repeated his question.

"We filed a report down at the station," replied Jared Smith, the man who had been speaking when Tyler returned to the table. "The sheriff wasn't too terribly concerned, but he wrote it down. Said he'd let me know if there were similar reports. I haven't heard a word."

"Problem is, our ranches and farms are so spread out. Folks don't know what's happening from location to location," added the second man, Hoss Johnson.

"My boss asked me to check around while I was on the poetry circuit," Clint said. "That's why I was askin'. There's more to this than just some teenagers messing around. One missing tank is a fluke maybe, but I'm thinkin' there's something more organized going on, especially after hearing y'all's stories."

"Your boss...?" Tyler asked, looking at Clint. He'd had him pegged as the lone wolf kind, living on the open range, breaking wild horses and writing verse alone at night by a campfire. Tyler had always had a romantic imagination as well as a weakness for lone wolves.

"I'm the foreman at Ransom Ranch over in Ransom Canyon. We breed Angus cattle. The tank that went missing contained prize bull semen worth upwards of ten thousand dollars. We've got insurance, but some of that stuff is irreplaceable. The boss is seriously pissed. I figured I might do some investigating of my own."

Tyler, while pleased to be assigned his first solo article with the poetry festival, smelled a more exciting story. What if there was more to this than just some kids on a lark, something bigger? He closed his eyes briefly, imagining his editor's surprise when he handed in a real investigative piece about a spate of bull semen thefts in West Texas. Maybe he'd even break the case himself. If Clint Darrow was amenable to his tagging along, that was. He decided to bide his time before asking if he could join the impromptu investigation. Hopefully he could get his editor's approval for a few more days out in the field for the project.

The men talked for a while longer, before drifting inside to listen to music and buy themselves more beer. After a while Huck took his leave, leaving Tyler alone with Clint Darrow. He sternly reminded himself again he was here to do a job, not pick up a cowboy. And as Clint had aptly pointed out to Huck, just because a guy was gay, didn't mean he was attracted to everything male. For all Tyler knew, Clint was in a relationship, or just plain not interested in what he probably thought of as some upstart city boy reporter.

He'd do his job and write up a solid piece for the magazine's arts and music section and then maybe there'd be an opportunity to talk about the missing tanks later. Clint Darrow would make a good addition to the festival article. Tyler had already interviewed two other cowboy poets during the course of the event, but knew Clint would be the one he featured.

"Say," Tyler ventured. "If it's not too late, can I still get that interview?"

"Sure." Clint nodded.

Tyler withdrew a small digital recorder from his shirt pocket. "Mind if I turn this on? Easier than jotting notes, if it's okay with you."

"No problem."

"I've done a little background research on you," he offered, hoping to both flatter the cowboy and show he'd done his homework. "You've made quite a name for yourself on the cowboy poetry circuit. You took first prize at the prestigious Cowboy Poetry Gathering in Lubbock last year."

Clint shrugged. "I don't do this for the prizes," he said, a smile ghosting its way across his face. "I do it because poetry is meant to be heard. I like the chance to share it with folks who actually want to hear it."

"I have to admit," Tyler said, "when I got this assignment, I didn't know a lot about the circuit. I grew up on a horse ranch not that far from here, so of course I was aware there are cowboy poets, but I didn't really know the history and all."

Clint nodded. "Long tradition, dating back as long as there's been cowboys, I'd reckon. Back when you had all them unemployed soldiers from the Civil War rounding up wild cattle and trailing them north, they'd settle 'round the campfire and recite stories for one another composed during long hours in the saddle, set to the rhyme of creaking leather and drumming hoof beats. I guess it's a kind of witnessing. I'm proud to be a part of it."

"That second poem you recited," Tyler dared. "The one about the wild horse. Something about it, I don't know…" he trailed off. He could feel the sexual tension buzzing between them, though he warned himself the odds were good it was entirely one-sided. Had Clint picked up on his cues, on the way he hadn't moved away when their thighs touched, even after Huck's remarks? A straight guy would have probably leaped away at that point, but Tyler hadn't budged. He pressed on, reminding himself he had a job to do. "I sensed a subtext. Were there layers beneath the spoken words—some kind of dual or hidden meaning?"

He shot a glance at Clint, whose direct gaze made Tyler's heart skitter around like a loose pinball. "That's one of the great things about poetry," Clint said. "Each person gets something different out of it, maybe something the poet never intended, but it's no less valid because of that. If anything, those added layers give the poetry more life and meaning. What was it, exactly, that you heard behind the words?" Clint's voice was low and raspy, as if it were laced with whiskey, smoke and hard living. There was a kind of power to it that drew Tyler and distracted him, despite his best effort to maintain his professional demeanor.

Tyler licked his lips, unable to look away from Clint's dark gaze, even if he had wanted to. "The reference to an exchange of power," he finally breathed, his words coming out in a whisper. Clint knew he was gay too. He was sure of it now. The small tape player whirred on, but Tyler knew he wasn't going to complete the interview just then. He could barely remember his own name, much less the questions he'd planned to ask.

His eyes still on Tyler's face, Clint dropped his hand to Tyler's thigh, his touch radiating like heat directly to Tyler's aching cock and balls. "Go on," Clint said softly. "Tell me more about what you heard in the poem." Tyler was aware suddenly of the silence in the courtyard. Other than a few stragglers smoking cigarettes along the fence, the place had emptied. Tyler supposed folks had gone inside to hear the music, or gone home now that the readings were over.

He closed his eyes, distracted by the rhythm of Clint's breath, the pitch of his voice, the feel of his hand still pressing against Tyler's denim-clad thigh, the fingers brushing carelessly close to his groin.

He opened his eyes and their gazes collided. When Tyler spoke, his voice came out gruff. He cleared his throat and tried again. "The image of submission, of the horse giving over its power to its master. I felt like maybe you were saying something more…" Tyler swallowed, unwilling to go on, afraid he'd already exposed too much of his closely held feelings.

"You're very perceptive." Clint tilted his head as he tightened his grip on Tyler's thigh. "I could be wrong. Lord knows it wouldn't be the first time. But I sense by your reaction that you identify with the wild stallion, the one who longs to be tamed by a real master."

"Oh," Tyler said, the word pulled from him. The night air was almost cool, but sweat prickled in his armpits as a shudder of pure, raw lust moved through his body.

"I take it that's a yes?" Clint covered Tyler's throbbing crotch with his large, strong hand.

Grateful for the semi-darkness that blanketed the courtyard, he thought about pulling away from Clint's forward touch, but found himself rooted to the spot. He opened his mouth to answer, but no words came.

They stood in the parking lot, their mutual decision to leave the bar together tacit but clear. Tyler followed Clint to a pickup truck, unable to deny the magnetic, almost overpowering pull of his attraction to this man who had somehow honed right in on his most secret thoughts and desires.

Not since the mess with Wayne Hurley that had sent Tyler running had he even allowed himself to think along these lines. ...*tamed by a real master*... Those fantasies, fueled by the quiet desperation of a lifetime of vague longing, had flared into a brief but powerful reality with Wayne. What they'd shared had been forbidden and, for Tyler, filled with shame, but charged with power just the same.

"I'm stayin' at the Motel Six, just down the road," Clint said. "I could use some company."

Tyler didn't reply. He felt like he was burning up. Desires he thought he'd left behind at the ranch six months before were fanned into flame by Clint's compelling presence. Though he wasn't sick, he could feel the flush moving over his skin like a fever. Clint stood loose and easy, as if he had all the time in the world. He waited a long beat before adding, "I knew it, before you even said a word. You've got that wild stallion inside you. But I can see it gives you no peace. You've been mishandled, I'd wager. You need gentlin' by a firm, sure hand."

Tyler tried to laugh but it came out hollow. "I don't know what the hell you're talking about." He'd meant to add a sneer to his voice, but heard instead the defensive protest in his tone, which even to his own ears lacked conviction.

"Sure you do. No cause to deny it. Not with me." Clint opened the passenger door to his truck and nodded an invitation toward the empty cab. He walked around the front of the truck and climbed into the driver's seat.

Tyler stood a moment, trying to tell himself he should bid this stranger who assumed way too much a good night, or at the very least tell him that he'd take his own car, thank you very much.

Clint started the engine, the barest hint of a smile moving over his face.

Tyler climbed in.

Chapter 2

Tyler stood in the middle of the motel room, which was lit by the eerie glow of the neon vacancy sign just outside the window. The air was hot and close in the small room. Tyler could feel the sweat breaking again beneath his arms and down his spine. He watched Clint move around the room, turning on a lamp, switching on the air conditioning unit, removing his cowboy hat and placing it on the bureau. There was a coil of rope beside the hat, the kind used for roping horses.

Clint approached him, standing so close Tyler could feel his breath on his cheek. "I want you," Clint murmured. He stepped back with that same maddening half smile he'd offered when they'd first met, and sat down on the only chair in the room, spreading his legs wide, cowboy boots firmly planted on the floor. He leaned back, putting his hands behind his head. Tyler resisted the primal impulse to fall to his knees between those long legs.

"Get nekkid," Clint ordered, his voice gentle but firm.

Tyler hesitated a moment, but decided that's what he'd come for—some casual sex with a hot cowboy. Why shouldn't he get naked? He was young and strong and had nothing to hide. With a shrug and a smile, he kicked off his boots and shucked out of his pants.

When Tyler was stripped bare, Clint got to his feet and walked around him in a little circle, trailing his fingers so that they were always brushing Tyler's skin. His touch left lines of heat as it moved over Tyler's chest, back, abs and stomach, inching downward toward Tyler's bobbing erection.

"Oh my," Clint said with a wolf's smile as he gripped the hard shaft. Tyler groaned, leaning into Clint's hold, his balls tight with need. He hadn't had sex in over a month, the last time being yet another casual, empty encounter with someone met over a beer, someone named Jeff or James, something with a J, he could no longer recall.

Clint stepped back, unbuttoning his shirt and tossing it aside, his agenda clearly the same as Tyler's. As he undressed, Tyler could see that his body was muscular and compact, with a cowboy's dark tan over his face, neck and arms. His chest was powerful and covered in dark curls that moved in a V down his sternum. He reached for Tyler, pulling him close. Their cocks collided as they moved, before lining up against their bellies, one beside the other, both hard as steel.

They were about the same height, just at six feet, though Tyler was broader where Clint was lean though muscular. When Clint leaned his head forward, Tyler expected their lips to meet. He found his own parting in anticipation, but instead Clint dipped his head. He nudged the skin at Tyler's neck with his teeth, biting just hard enough to get Tyler's full attention. At the same time, Clint reached for his bare ass, gripping and kneading the cheeks with strong, sure hands.

Tyler reached for Clint as well, pulling his body hard against him, a light sweat mingling between them despite the window unit's wheezing efforts to cool the room. Tyler's body was humming in anticipation, his cock throbbing, his fingers tingling as they moved over Clint's skin, feeling the flexed muscle rippling beneath.

There was something about this man—he'd felt it the moment he'd begun speaking on the stage and its grip hadn't left him the whole evening. He exuded a kind of quiet, confident power—not the sort that shouted, but the kind that only needed to incline the head to make others pay attention and obey.

They fondled each other, fingers stroking, cocks pressed hard against bellies, feet planted firm as they pulled each other closer. Tyler tried to tell himself this was nothing more than a quick, easy fuck with a hot near-stranger. He'd had a couple of beers and that, combined with the hot summer night and the near constant of his loneliness, had made his blood flow faster, that was all. Tonight was about sex for its own sake, without emotional involvement or commitment or any ulterior motive. That's all he needed, he told himself. That's all he wanted.

And yet Tyler couldn't seem to catch his breath. His heart was beating fast, a steady tapping against his ribs, and his knees wobbled, as if he'd just received shocking news. When Clint pressed against his shoulder, it seemed only natural to sink down to the floor at Clint's feet.

Impulsively, he wrapped his arms around Clint's thickly-muscled thighs and rubbed his cheek along the man's rigid shaft. He turned his head, licking a line down the smooth skin, tracing a long bulging vein with his tongue.

Clint gently pushed Tyler away from his hard cock, angling his body in such a way that his heavy balls were thrust toward Tyler's parted lips instead. "Show me how much you want it. Go on." Tyler leaned forward hungrily, tonguing the silky skin. Eagerly he sucked each ball into his mouth, taking his time as he savored Clint's spicy-sweet scent. He felt Clint's hand on the back of his head as he pressed his balls against Tyler's open mouth, his cock still out of reach. His hand was strong and sure as he held Tyler in place.

Tyler pulled back, disconcerted, unwilling to admit how hard it made his cock to be held in position like that. To distract himself, he ran his lips over Clint's right thigh, licking the salty skin. Lowering his head and closing his eyes, he licked down Clint's leg. When his tongue touched the thickened, raised skin just above Clint's knee, he opened his eyes, feeling the dense ridge of scar tissue with his fingers, recalling

Clint's limp.

"What happened?"

"Amateur rodeo back when I was a kid. Bull ridin'."

An image of Clint astride the back of a powerful bull, and then tossed down onto the hard packed dirt, gored by the bull's sharp horns, the blood gushing, the crowd letting out a chorus of shocked dismay, rippled through Tyler's imagination.

"You got gored?" he whispered in horrified awe.

Clint shook his head with a self-deprecating grin. "Nah, nothin' so glamorous. My third time out I got pinned to the wall by a pissed-off steer before I even got to mount him for my eight seconds of glory. Tore up my leg on a wooden post and that was the end of my rodeo career, such as it was."

Tyler ran his fingers over the smooth, ridged scar tissue and leaned forward, lightly licking the flesh with his tongue. His cock was aching. Still on his hands and knees, he lifted his head, craning toward Clint's bobbing shaft and swaying balls with parted lips.

Clint was watching him, a strange fire behind his eyes making them glitter beneath the hooded lids. Then he bent forward, and Tyler felt the older man's calloused hands moving along his spine, his long arms reaching steadily downwards. Tyler was nearly shaking by the time those hands finally moved over his ass, stroking the flesh, circling toward the center. Clint pressed the fat head of his engorged cock between Tyler's willing lips as his fingers played along the cleft between Tyler's ass cheeks.

Tyler moaned against the shaft, unable to stop himself from pressing against the finger poised at his entrance. It eased inside him as Tyler sucked eagerly on Clint's cock. He alternated between sucking Clint's cock as deep as he could and thrusting back toward the hard digit pressing its way inside him. He was momentarily dismayed when Clint pulled his cock from Tyler's mouth and the finger from his ass. He forgot his dismay, however, as Clint pressed his head, gently but firmly, toward the floor, which in turn forced Tyler's bare ass up like an offering.

Keeping one hand firmly on the back of Tyler's neck, Clint's other hand returned to his ass, spreading the cheeks and inserting one and then two fingers into Tyler's stretching orifice.

"This is what you need," he said in a low drawl.

Tyler groaned, his cock throbbing between his legs. As much as it disconcerted him, something about being held down in this way, forced into such a submissive posture, was almost enough to make him come on the spot. He realized his mouth was resting on top of one of Clint's bare feet. Without consciously thinking about what he was doing, Tyler began to kiss the top of Clint's foot.

Despite promises to himself to keep this encounter light and easy, Tyler could feel the pull of Clint's powerful presence. He drifted into that secret, dark place, pulled down by Clint's sure touch and the unspoken power that shimmered between them and settled over Tyler like a finely spun web. As Clint continued to finger and fondle Tyler's spread ass, Tyler let go, losing himself in a deep sensual slide.

"You look good down there on your knees, boy," Clint said in that low, sexy rasp. When the words penetrated the sensual fog that had filled Tyler's brain, it was as if the door to a secret room had been pulled suddenly open and the lights flicked on, harsh and unwelcome.

Tyler sat back abruptly on his haunches, wrapping his arms protectively around his chest. "I'm not into that stuff," he muttered, angry at himself. Hadn't he sworn to steer well clear of this kind of man? Danger signs flashed in his head. Somehow he needed to move the action back to sex, pure and simple. Hadn't the disastrous relationship with Wayne taught him that?

Clint stepped back, his arms falling away from Tyler's body. He lifted his eyebrows, offering a sardonic smile.

Tyler closed his eyes, consciously pushing away the memory of Wayne slamming him against the wall in the tack room. Yeah, the sting of the whip against his bare ass had been exciting, but he could have done without the hard punches to his chest and shoulders and the careless slaps to his face afterward. Though he'd come to hate the man, he'd still loved the rough play, as much as he wanted to deny it.

But despite his powerful reaction to what Wayne had offered, in the six months since he'd been gone he'd managed to keep those feelings at bay, hidden away even from himself—until now.

Tyler could feel his face burning. The damn thing of it was, he loved being there at Clint's feet. No, love wasn't the word. He craved it. The shrouded embers of his lust had burst into flame once more and it was raging beyond his control. When he felt like this, common sense just flew out the window, even when he knew better.

He looked away, blowing out a breath, angry at himself and his weakness. He needed to get out of there. This had been a mistake. He looked toward the pile of clothing, his legs tensing beneath him in preparation of rising. He owed this man nothing.

He glanced at Clint, who was watching him with a bemused expression. "What's goin' on between those ears of yours? Ain't no shame in being somebody's boy, Tyler. In fact, with the right man, there ain't nothin' finer."

Tyler drew in a sharp breath. Who the hell was this cowboy, who seemed almost privy to his secret thoughts? He'd seemed so fine and upright, but Tyler had learned from experience men were not always what they seemed.

Wayne had acted much like any other hired hand on the ranch, a little swagger, a little bluster, but no real hint of the cruel streak hidden beneath the surface. Who was to say Clint Darrow was any different? Better to get while the gettin' was good.

"Look, I'm sorry but this is a mistake. I need to go." Tyler rose, his eye on his jeans as he turned his back on the cowboy. He heard Clint moving behind him, but continued forward, determined to dress and leave before things went any further.

He was reaching down for his clothing when suddenly sturdy rope was slung over his head and quickly tightened around his body, pinning his arms to his sides. "What the hell—" he cried, confused and flustered.

"You ain't goin' no place, Tyler Sutton. Not till you prove to me this ain't what you need." Clint was behind him, pulling the strong, soft nylon rope tight around Tyler's upper body before he even realized what was happening.

"Goddamn it," Tyler cursed, jerking hard against the restraints, but Clint had been quick, and the knots he was tying were at Tyler's back. "Let me go. You can't keep me here by force."

Clint's voice was low and sexy in Tyler's ear. "Well, I can, but I don't plan to. No. Whatever you give me tonight, you give me because you want to. I'm just slowin' you down a little, is all. Giving you a chance to stop running and take stock of just what it is you're runnin' from."

Tyler wrenched away, twisting to view his captor, his heart beating high in his throat. "This is crazy. What the fuck do you think you're doing?"

"Nothin' you don't want." Clint glanced down at Tyler's cock, which was hard as a rock. Clint had a second piece of rope in his hands, and before Tyler could stop him, he'd stepped behind him again, grabbing Tyler's wrists in a surprisingly strong grip, and pulled them behind his back. In seconds he'd looped and knotted the rope around them.

Clint moved around to face him again, his cock as hard as Tyler's own. He swept Tyler's bare body with a long, appraising gaze, his tongue appearing between his parted lips. "You look mighty fine, boy. Tell me now that you don't like it. Tell me you weren't born to kneel at somebody's feet, ready and willin' to take what they give you. Tell me you hate to be tied up. Tell me all that and I'll let you loose."

Tyler opened his mouth to say just that, but somehow the words stuck in his throat. Clint chuckled softly. They were standing close by the bed, and a single push made Tyler lose his footing. He fell heavily against the mattress. Clint gently rolled him onto his stomach, climbed over him and straddled his hips.

He stretched out over Tyler, pinning him with his solid weight, his cock hard against the small of Tyler's back. Tyler felt his teeth again at his neck, and then his tongue, soft and warm as it licked upward toward his ear. Clint reached beneath Tyler, finding and gripping his cock, which was throbbing despite his predicament.

Tyler tried to jerk away. "You let me up, goddamn you," he cried breathlessly, twisting beneath the strong man on top of him. "I don't do this. I told you, I ain't nobody's boy. Damn it, let me up."

"You sure?" Clint's voice was a low purr in Tyler's ear. He kissed a line down Tyler's neck with soft but insistent lips. As he stroked his cock with one hand, the other found Tyler's right nipple, which he pulled and rolled between strong fingers.

"Oh, god," Tyler gasped, aware he was seconds away from orgasm. He tried to hold on to the outrage at what Clint had done, trussing him up like some kind of stubborn colt, but it burned away before the liquid fire roiling in his veins. His heart was pounding so hard he thought it might lift him clear off the bed.

He wanted to deny how good it felt. "Damn…," he managed. "Don't…," he struggled to catch his breath, his cock near to bursting. "Clint…," he gasped, trying to draw on the last remnants of his righteous anger to give weight to his words. But the lust boiling in his gut, coupled with the steady, perfect grip of Clint's strong hand on his cock and the insistent fingers teasing his nipple were too much to fight.

"Please," he gasped, no longer certain what he was pleading for or against. "Please...yes...please..."

"Ah, fuck," he groaned at last, giving up all pretense of resistance as his body went rigid and streams of hot ejaculate were expertly milked from his cock. Despite the ropes, because of the ropes... Damn it to hell, he didn't know, he didn't want to know, but oh, oh, oh it was so fucking good.

~*~

Clint untied the rope and tossed it aside, half-expecting Tyler to leap up, still pretending outrage. But Tyler didn't try to get away. Instead he snuggled back against Clint, letting a long contented sigh escape his lips. Clint wrapped his arms around him, reaching to stroke and soothe the nipple he'd been pulling and twisting a moment before. He'd taken a gamble with the rope, but apparently it had paid off. If nothing else, Tyler was still there, in his arms. Though he wasn't yet absolutely certain, Clint was pretty sure there was more here than mere sexual masochism.

He had sensed Tyler's potential for submission at the poetry reading, but he'd felt it even stronger when they'd come back to the room. He'd seen it in the way Tyler's eyes had dilated and the sweat had appeared on his upper lip when Clint had sprawled on the chair, silently daring Tyler to kneel before him. He'd felt it in the hungry, almost desperate way Tyler had worshipped his cock and balls, and then bowed his head, raining kisses over the tops of Clint's feet.

He had responded in kind, moved by Tyler's exuberant attentions. The boy seemed to want so very much what he was offering. There was a potential connection here—the chance to reach for something he hadn't realized he'd given up on, until faced with its possibility. Still, this colt was skittish and would require some gentling. As much as he wanted him, Clint knew better than to move too fast, not with the likes of Tyler Sutton.

For reasons Clint had yet to tease out of him, Tyler was in denial about his true and most basic impulses. While Clint had no doubt that in Tyler he had found a submissive, he'd learned all too well over the years that just because a body knew a thing, that didn't mean it was easy to act on it. Tyler was as resistant as a calf being pulled unwilling into the rodeo ring.

For a moment he regretted his rough treatment with the rope. Hopefully it hadn't been too much, too fast. "You okay, Ty?" he whispered softly, drawing Tyler closer against him.

"Yeah," Tyler murmured, pressing back against Clint's erection so that it took every ounce of control not to take him then and there. If he didn't care whether Tyler stayed or went afterward, he might have done just that. But something held him back. Maybe, he admitted, there was more here than just a one-night-stand.

What was really going on with the boy? He was clearly into what Clint was offering, but at the same time, he seemed ashamed. Maybe it was simpler than that.

"You out, Ty?" Clint asked gently.

"Huh?"

"Out of the closet."

"Oh. Yeah. I guess. I mean, I don't hide it, not anymore."

"Not anymore…" Clint prompted.

Tyler frowned. "It's one thing being openly gay in Austin. Back on my father's horse ranch was another story, as I'm sure you know. I'm the only son of a proud line of Suttons. No pansies in the Sutton line, no siree, Bob. I learned early on to keep myself to myself, if you know what

I mean."

"So you left in order to come out without payin' a price with your family? Is that it?" Clint had a strong feeling there was more to this story than Tyler was sharing, but what?

"I don't want to go there," Tyler retorted sharply, his body stiffening. "Some other time, maybe."

Stung by the sharpness of Tyler's tone, Clint reached for Tyler's shoulders, which had gone tight along with his voice. "Sure," he said. "I apologize. Sometimes I put my nose where it don't belong. Don't pay me no mind." He massaged Tyler's shoulders, relieved when he felt the tension easing from the bunched muscles.

"That feels good," Tyler offered, by way of apology, it seemed to Clint, for snapping at him. Clint kept up the massage, ignoring his erection as best he could for the time being.

"You know," he said finally, as Tyler leaned back into him with a contented sigh, "I found out a long time ago it wasn't worth it to fight other folks, but most especially myself, over who and what I am. I'm hardwired this way and there ain't a thing I can do about it. I'll be forty before this year is out and life is just too damn short to keep up the lies just so other folks feel more comfortable."

"How's that go over on your ranch? You carry a loaded gun or what?" Tyler asked, the bitterness again creeping into his tone.

Clint laughed. "Them as has business knowin', they know I'm gay, includin' the boss. He's fine with it, so long as I do my job. The ranch hands, they work for me, and if they pull any crap, they find out pretty damn fast they got the wrong pig by the tail." He paused, adding, "I guess my point is, *I'm* comfortable with who and what I am. In the long run, that's all that really matters."

Tyler said nothing. It was good to have him in his arms, but Clint wanted more. He wanted, somehow, to reach him. He offered, "When I'm up on the stage I try to find that one person in the audience I can relate to. Someone who seems to be gettin' it, if you know what I mean. Someone who catches the deeper meanin' beneath the spoken word."

"Yeah," Tyler said softly, and Clint could feel him listening intently now.

"Tonight that was you," Clint continued. "Even before I knew you were gay. Even before I knew you were submissive..." He let the words hang, waiting for Tyler's protest. His heart tightened and increased its pace when Tyler, while not overtly admitting it, didn't deny it either.

Encouraged, Clint continued. "You honed in on the layers hidden beneath the rhymes about tamin' wild horses. You connected to the deeper aspects of my verse. That means a lot to me, Tyler. It binds us in a special way. Leastways it does for me."

Tyler twisted toward him, his cornflower blue eyes locking with Clint's. "Just because a man understands a thing, that doesn't have to mean he's into it."

"You askin' me or tellin' me?" Clint pondered if he should be exasperated or amused at Tyler's continued resistance. He decided to go with the latter.

"I dunno," Tyler mumbled, shifting back so his ass was again spooned against Clint's hard cock.

Clint began to move slowly, rubbing his aching cock gently against the cleft of Tyler's ass. "To answer your question, no, a man don't have to be into somethin' to get it. But by the same token, when a man's heart is poundin' and he's gaspin' for breath while on his knees kissing the feet of another, it don't take no rocket scientist to figure out there's somethin' going on."

Recalling Tyler's strong reaction earlier, Clint reached around his body to stroke Tyler's nipples, his touch at first feather-light. They quickly hardened, encouraging Clint to pull and twist the nubbins until he drew a moan from Tyler's lips. Oh yes, the boy needed this, and Clint needed to give it to him. His cock throbbed against Tyler's ass.

"You need this, you know you do. And I can give it to you," Clint whispered, twisting harder.

"Yes," Tyler hissed, his admission sending a jolt of lust straight to Clint's aching cock. He couldn't wait another second. Letting go of Tyler's nipples, Clint reached back toward the night table where he'd left his wallet.

"I'm gonna claim you now. We'll take it easy and slow, but I got to have you." He pulled a condom from his wallet and tore the wrapper, pulling back long enough to slide it over his shaft. It was pre-lubricated, and he licked his fingers and rubbed the tip to make it easier for Tyler to handle.

Tyler grunted as the head of Clint's cock popped inside. Clint, now in total control of Tyler's body, pulled him gently back as he shifted to make the penetration easier. He kissed him hard, and Tyler kissed him back, panting against his mouth.

"I got to have you," Clint repeated, as he pushed himself slowly into the hot, tight passage. "I got to make you mine."

"Oh," Tyler moaned softly, pressing back to receive him.

Once Clint was fully inside, he began to move, slowly at first, letting the boy adjust. When Tyler began to push back against him, Clint reached down to grab Tyler's cock, which had hardened, despite the recent orgasm. As his hand closed over the rigid shaft, he heard a groan and realized it was his own.

How long had it been since he'd felt this way with someone new? His mind flickered and stuttered as if losing its signal, and he gave himself at last fully to what his body was experiencing. He thrust into Tyler, holding him in place and riding him hard.

He pulled Tyler's cock in time to his own savage, primal thrusts. He wanted to slow down, to be gentler, but his body would not listen or obey. He almost thought he could hear the roar of the avalanche of his impending orgasm, gathering force as it prepared to tumble through him.

"Oh god," Tyler cried. "I'm coming. Oh…" His spasms dragged Clint over the edge, his body shaking with seismic force as he shuddered and moaned into Tyler's neck.

He fell back against the mattress, their sweat-slick bodies separating. Tyler at once curled into him, resting his head against Clint's chest. Clint drifted a moment, or was it longer…? When his heart had slowed enough to where he could catch his breath and regain the use of his muscles, Clint reached down, stroking the wet, matted hair from Tyler's damp forehead.

Tyler opened his eyes, staring up at Clint with such naked adoration that, had Clint been the blushing kind, he would have colored to the tips of his ears. Leaning up slightly, Tyler kissed Clint's chin and smiled the smile of a baby drunk on mother's milk. A feeling of overwhelming tenderness swept through Clint, leaving him, for that brief moment, utterly defenseless.

"Thank you," Tyler whispered, so softly Clint wondered if he'd only imagined it. He experienced a sudden sense of loss. It had been far too long since he'd felt that eager puppy spark, either in himself or from another. When had he traded in the promise of that kind of wild, powerful love for a life of placid contentment?

Clint realized with a jolt that, if things had gone according to plan, he would be in the arms of his familiar, tried and true old friend and sometimes lover, as comfortable as an old quilt, and about as exciting. These poetry festivals and readings, away from the ranch and his usual life, were a good opportunity for a little stolen sweetness, but in the end, that's all it was.

Or was this time different? It was crazy even to speculate. And yet the aching tenderness for the young man cradled in his arms still lingered. Something in Tyler called to him like a lone coyote's howl, plaintive and filled with longing.

Would he be able to break through the walls Tyler had erected between himself and his desires?

Chapter 3

"Okay, we're good to go. The owner says you can leave your car here at the honky-tonk over the next few days. Everything all set on your end?" Clint slid back into the booth seat opposite Tyler, who was sipping coffee, his runny eggs and sausage patties barely touched. Beneath the smell of bacon grease remained the lingering odor of stale beer and whiskey from countless nights of cowboys and ranchers kicking back at the end of a long day. The bar doubled as a diner by day, and while the food wasn't terribly good, it was cheap, and the coffee was hot and fresh.

"Yeah. I got the go-ahead from my editor to follow the story. I really appreciate the chance to tag along." To hear the two of them talk, one might have supposed they were casual acquaintances. The heat and passion they'd shared the night before was cloaked by the long-ingrained habit of keeping their true feelings and orientation close to the vest—a survival instinct as natural to most gay men in rural Texas as breathing.

"Glad for the company," Clint said. He eyed the younger man over the rim of his mug. He was fresh scrubbed from their shared shower, his hair still damp. He looked younger than his thirty years, though he looked tired. Which was understandable, as Clint had kept him up half the night, unable to keep his hands off the boy.

It had been so long, too long, since he'd connected not only physically, but mentally with someone. When Tyler had knelt at his feet, his eyes lowered and his face flushed, the need to submit had shone from him like a light, its beacon calling Clint out of self-imposed darkness that had gone on for too long.

And when Tyler had licked down Clint's leg, stopping to kiss and explore the scar with such reverence and innocent adoration, something had snapped with a kind of sweet pain in Clint's heart.

Again Clint found himself wondering, as he had the night before, when that shiny-new possibility of love had slipped away from the realm of his day-to-day life. Had he ever been as eager and desperately excited as Tyler had been the night before?

And yet beneath the excitement, or perhaps overlaying it like a blanket tossed over a campfire, something had held Tyler back. *I'm not into that stuff,* was all he would say, but Clint could hear the unspoken murmur of the back story beneath those few cryptic words.

While he didn't sense that Tyler had major issues with being gay, it was the submissive aspect that had him troubled. Was Clint the man to teach him otherwise? Did he even want to? After all, his love life, if not exactly tilt-o-whirl exciting, was steady and comfortable, a known quantity. Did he really want to upset the balance he'd created over the years?

Even as these practical, rational thoughts entered his head, Clint rejected them. For what is life without risk? If you never reached for a thing, how could you hope to capture it?

Tyler had expressed an interest in coming along on Clint's informal investigation of the missing bull semen tanks. They would spend a few days traveling over the West Texas plains, checking out the ranches and farms that had reported thefts to see what they could find out. In a few days Tyler would return to Austin, Clint would return to Ransom Canyon.

But was that what he wanted? Here sat the sexiest, most exciting guy to cross his path in years, maybe ever, and he was acting like things were over before they'd barely had a chance to begin. Since when did Clint Darrow give up before the bull was even out of the chute?

The waitress, a petite woman in a tight pink waitress uniform, set the bill on the table. "Y'all don't be strangers, hear?" She patted Clint on the shoulder and Clint offered a distracted smile. Both men reached for their wallets at the same time, reminding Clint of the old westerns on TV where the hero and the villain reach for their guns, each determined to draw first.

Tyler was quicker, his hand covering the slip of paper as he said, "I got it. Expense account. The magazine will pay the tab." Clint could see by the look in his eye and the set of his jaw that Tyler was bound and determined to get the check, as if by doing so he was proving some unspoken point. Clint shrugged and pushed his wallet back into his pocket as Tyler withdrew some bills and placed them on the table.

They stood, each taking a last sip of coffee. "Guess we'll get this show on the road," Clint said, though as he glanced at Tyler, the tug in his loins told him he'd rather go back to the motel room instead and pick up where they'd left off.

"Where we headed first?" Tyler asked, as they climbed into either side of the truck cab.

"Blake's place is closest. It's about two hours from here, give or take."

They were quiet as Clint maneuvered out of the parking lot and began to drive down the county road. Eventually Tyler pulled out his digital cassette recorder and continued the interview for the festival. Clint answered as best he could, the thought that he'd be featured in some slick magazine amusing to him and also, if he were honest, kind of exciting.

Music was playing softly on the radio. Hoping to draw Tyler out some, Clint said, "You mentioned you was raised on a ranch in these parts. You still got family here?"

"Double S Horse Ranch, 'bout fifty miles south of here. My father owns and runs the place. For a while I thought I'd want to take it over someday."

Something in Tyler's tone warned Clint to back off, but he persisted. "I've heard of that ranch. Got a good reputation. So what made you change your mind?"

When Tyler didn't answer, Clint glanced away from the road, taking in the hunch of Tyler's shoulders and scowl on his face. Switching tacks, he said, "You must 'a gone to college to be workin' for a big magazine like *Lone Star Monthly*, with an expense account and all."

"College isn't always what it's cracked up to be, but yeah, I went. Got a degree in animal science from A&M, with a minor in journalism. Good thing, it turns out." He gave a bitter laugh.

"So your leavin' wasn't entirely your decision…?" Clint let the question hang.

"If you don't mind, I'd rather not talk about all that just now, if it's all the same to you." Tyler's voice was tight.

"Sure, no problem." Clint focused on the road, feeling something inside close up just a little bit. He should have known better than to press.

They arrived at Blake's place by late morning. Clint had met Seth Blake on a number of occasions, along with his wife, Mary. He'd called ahead to ask if he could stop by and now Mary, a tall willowy woman in her late fifties came out of the farm house, wiping her hands on a large apron that covered her T-shirt and shorts.

"Howdy Clint," she said. "You're looking fine as ever."

Clint smiled. "Nice to see you, Mary. This here's Tyler Sutton, a friend of mine all the way from Austin."

Mary smiled at Tyler, inclining her head in welcome. "It's right nice to meet you." Turning to Clint, she added, "How's Joe and Tildy? I've been meaning to have them over to supper one of these days but time just gets away from a body."

Clint filled her in on the health of his boss and the boss's wife and they exchanged other small talk for a while about mutual acquaintances. Finally Mary said, "Seth's out at the milking barn. He said to go on back when you got here."

Clint nodded his thanks and the two of them walked along the path toward the barns, the pungent smell of cow manure and fresh cut hay wafting toward them in the warm air. Seth was in with his dairy cows. He was a large man with plenty of weight around his middle.

"Clint Darrow!" he exclaimed, stepping out of the barn and moving toward them as he wiped a bandana over his sweating brow. "Good to see you again, buddy. It's been too long." They shook hands and Clint introduced Tyler.

They exchanged small talk about the price of milk, the state of ranching and innocuous gossip about mutual friends before Clint ventured to the reason he'd come. "I was talkin' to Hoss Johnson and Jared Smith over at Jack's honky-tonk last night. They mentioned you were one of the folks as had some bull semen go missing. We had a pretty significant theft back at our place a few days back. I thought, seein' as I was in the area, I'd come check it out. See if we could maybe piece together some kind of pattern."

"It was the damnedest thing." Seth knitted his brow, his face clouding. "I've been in the cattle business for nigh on thirty years, and I ain't never had nobody steal bull semen before. It's not like our semen is even valuable. Just basic seed to keep my cows breeding when we don't have a bull handy. I might not have even noticed it was missin', except Doc Crawford was here the other day to do a regular check and he noticed one of the cows was showin' signs of goin' into heat. I went to fetch one of the liquid nitrogen canisters and damn if two of them hadn't gone missin'. Them canisters don't come cheap neither."

The three of them talked for a while about the possibilities, speculating what might have happened. Seth tried to think if there'd been any mysterious strangers prowling round the ranch lately, but came up with nothing. Tyler scribbled on his notepad and Clint found himself hoping they'd solve this mystery, not just to recover the stolen property, but so Tyler would have a good story for his magazine.

A bell began to ring, the kind used in old one-room school houses to call the children in from recess. Seth looked toward the house. "Day starts at dawn. We eat early 'round here. I hope you got time to join us for lunch."

Clint glanced at his watch. It was a little past eleven. Though they weren't really on any schedule, Clint was possessive of his time with Tyler, not certain how much longer they had together. He didn't want to spend an extra moment in the company of others, except as it pertained to the investigation. "We got a kind of late start," he said, smiling apologetically. "If we're goin' to cover more ground before nightfall, we best be movin' on." Tyler nodded his agreement, which pleased Clint, though he warned himself not to assume it meant anything.

"Suit yourself." Seth patted his ample gut. "More for me. Mary makes a mighty fine brisket."

The three of them walked back to the house, where Mary, too, tried to get them to stay for the midday meal. They again declined politely, but accepted the sandwiches she insisted on making them for the road.

Along the highway Clint pulled in at a gas station and filled the truck's tank while Tyler waited in the cab, checking his cell phone voice mail, since reception was spotty out in the country. Clint went inside to pay and came out with a small Styrofoam cooler he'd stocked with ice and soda. He put the cooler on the floor by Tyler's feet, keeping out two bottles. He held one of the bottles toward Tyler. "Thirsty?"

Tyler took the bottle, examining it with a low, appreciative whistle. "Dr. Pepper, huh? I grew up on this stuff. I haven't seen glass bottles like this in years."

Clint smiled back. "You got to know where to look." He held up a bottle, the old-fashioned eight-ounce kind, the thick glass tinted green. "Best soda on the planet earth. Puts all others to shame."

"Where we headed now?" Tyler asked, as he twisted open his bottle.

"Harding Ranch is a couple hours from here. I figured we could stop for lunch somewhere along the way. Take our time." He glanced at Tyler, enjoying the sight of his Adam's apple bobbing as he tipped the bottle and drank. Tyler was wearing a button-down shirt, the sleeves rolled just below the elbow, several buttons open to reveal his chest, smooth save for a light down of golden-blond hair.

They listened to country music, keeping the conversation light, though a steady, undeniable sexual tension hummed between them right along with the torque of the truck engine.

After about an hour, Clint pointed toward a sign that indicated a rest area. The area contained a small cement building with restrooms and vending machines. Picnic tables were scattered out back beneath shade trees.

The parking lot contained a few cars and trucks, as well as some eighteen-wheelers. Folks were seated at various tables enjoying their lunches. A few children were running between the trees, laughing and calling to each other.

After they used the facilities, Clint and Tyler settled at an empty table, seating themselves on opposite sides. They ate their sandwiches, neither saying much. The day had been cloudy, and getting more so as the afternoon progressed, the heavy fat underbellies of the clouds darkening with potential rain.

The clouds parted for a moment, a shaft of sunlight penetrating the foliage overhead, illuminating Tyler's features in soft, buttery gold. He glanced up at Clint at that moment, a tentative smile moving over his lips and Clint realized he was smiling too, just for the sheer pleasure of looking at the handsome man sitting across from him. His cock was apparently appreciating the view as well; he could feel it lengthening, the balls tightening beneath it.

A twinge of pain moved through his knee and he shifted as a sudden, deliciously evil idea moved into his head. Extending his leg, he said, "I need to stretch out a bit." He positioned his leg so that his booted foot rested between Tyler's legs on the bench. He pressed the sole of his boot lightly against Tyler's bulge.

"Hey!" Tyler said, his eyes skittering from side to side at the people nearby. No one was close enough to overhear them, or really see what was going on beneath the table, but Clint could sense Tyler's sudden panic.

He offered a slow smile. Tyler started to pull back, but Clint's words stopped him. "You stay put, boy. I'm just restin' my bum leg." He pressed harder, the point of his boot digging into Tyler's crotch. A flush had started up Tyler's cheeks and his hands were clenched in fists on the table, but he didn't move.

He glanced around, swiveling his head as he swallowed nervously. "Focus on me," Clint admonished gently. "Only on me. Forget about them other folk. They don't exist." Tyler turned his head back toward Clint. His eyes were wide, the pupils dilated and he'd caught his lower lip between his teeth. Clint could feel Tyler's agitation, and his excitement.

"I want you hard," Clint told him. "Is your cock hard, boy?"

Tyler nodded, swallowing again.

"Speak up, boy. I didn't hear you." Clint pressed harder against Tyler's crotch. Tyler winced but didn't pull away.

"Yeah," Tyler managed.

Clint nodded. He kept his foot there, watching the conflict of emotions move over Tyler's face. He both liked and didn't like what Clint was doing to him. The fact he was staying put said more than any protests could have.

Satisfied, Clint let his leg fall. He stood, grabbing their trash and the empty soda bottles. "Let's go."

"I can't. Not quite yet."

Clint suppressed a smile, pretending he didn't understand. "Sure you can. Just stand up and walk. Easy as pie."

Tyler's flush darkened. "I can't. Folks will see…"

Clint laughed, a small, low growl of mirth. "You think too much of yourself, boy. Ain't nobody lookin' at you but me. And I like what I see. Very much. So move that hot ass of yours to the truck. Now." He added steel to his tone, the same steel he used when admonishing some lazy ranch hand.

Tyler stood, the bulge at his crotch leaving no doubt as to his state of arousal. They walked toward the truck, Clint taking his time, Tyler moving quickly in front of him. Once back in the cab, Clint started the engine and eased the truck out of its parking spot in front of the restrooms. Instead of driving back out onto the highway, he rolled the truck down to the back of the rest area, parking it beside a clump of bushes, partially obscured by two large dumpsters. They were mostly hidden from view, though it was still public enough to add a hint of danger to what Clint had in mind.

"Why're we parking here?" Tyler asked, glancing nervously around them.

Clint didn't answer. He reached into the cooler and pulled out an icy cold bottle of Dr. Pepper. Idling the engine, he turned to face Tyler. "Open your zipper and pull out that hard cock for me."

Tyler hesitated, licking his lips.

"Go on," Clint urged. "Do what I tell you."

He waited for the protest, but was pleased when, instead, Tyler shifted, lifting his hips as he unzipped his jeans. He reached into the fly of his underwear and pulled out the rigid shaft, glancing nervously out the windows.

"Someone's gonna see," he murmured anxiously.

"You let me worry about that. You just look at me and do what I say." Tyler was breathing a little too fast and again his lower lip was caught between his teeth, but he didn't argue. He locked eyes with Clint. Clint could feel his fire, which matched Clint's own.

"Sit on your hands," Clint ordered. "And keep 'em there, no matter what I do. You hear?"

Tyler slid his hands beneath his thighs, his cock bobbing at his groin. Clint reached for him, pressing his fingers in past the cotton of Tyler's underwear. He cupped and gently yanked Tyler's balls out of his underwear.

"Jesus, Clint," Tyler groaned. "Someone's gonna see."

"Shh," Clint replied. He fondled Tyler's balls and cock, his own cock pressing hard against his jeans. "Close your eyes."

Tyler waited a beat before obeying, but then his eyes fluttered shut, thick golden lashes shadowing his cheekbones. Taking the cold bottle of soda, Clint pressed it against Tyler's cock and balls.

Tyler gasped, his eyes flying open. "What the fuck…?" His protest was belied by the fact that he stayed in position, hands firmly beneath his legs. The state of his cock was telling as well, still hard as bone.

"Take it for me, boy. It's what I want. Sufferin' is good for the soul. Suffer for me." Tyler shuddered as Clint moved the cold glass over his cock and balls, but still he stayed in position.

Clint moved the bottle away, reaching for Tyler's shaft with his hand. He gripped it and pulled upward, drawing a groan from Tyler's lips. He played with Tyler's cock, alternating between the cold bottle and the hot, tight grip of his hand. Pushing the cooler lid aside, he grabbed a handful of ice and held it for several seconds before dropping it. When he cupped Tyler's balls with his freezing fingers, Tyler winced and drew in a sharp breath, jerking upright.

Clint kept his icy fingers on Tyler's balls while he stroked him with the other hand until Tyler fell back limp against the seat, his breathing ragged, his chest heaving. "I want you to come for me," Clint told him. "Somebody might come by. Somebody might see you. That don't matter a lick, you hear? You're gonna come for me because that's what I want, and more important, it's what you want. You showed me last night with your actions that you were born to serve, no matter how much you tried to deny it with your words, and now I'm goin' to prove it to you."

Clint pulled his hand away long enough to spit on his fingers and reached again for Tyler's shaft, gliding up and down with a firm, steady stroke. Tyler responded with muffled grunts and sighs, arching his body toward Clint's hand, his own hands still pinned beneath him. "Jesus, Clint," he murmured. "I'm gonna come."

"Good. That's what I want," Clint answered. Clint placed the still cold glass bottle against Tyler's balls as he continued to stroke his cock.

Tyler gasped and shuddered, his eyes opening as he turned to face Clint with a pleading expression. "I can't," Tyler groaned, shrinking back from the cold glass. "Not with that on me."

"Do it," Clint commanded. Keeping the bottle in place, Clint jerked steadily at Tyler's cock. The combination of heat, friction, cold and wet, along with the sensual overlay of his dominating words, would soon overload Ty's senses and send him over the edge. "Work through the discomfort. Focus on the orgasm. Come in spite of the cold. Come because I want you to."

Tyler's eyes slid shut again, his head falling back as his lips parted. He was panting, his body tensing. A man was approaching the area from a distance, a large trash bag in his hands, no doubt heading for the dumpsters.

"Come for me, boy," Clint urged. "Now."

Tyler arched forward with a small cry, his body spasming as ribbons of creamy white jism splattered the dash board. Clint waited as long as he dared, savoring the sight of the spent, sexy man beside him, his chest heaving, his cock dripping. Clint was aching to fuck him. He wanted nothing more at that moment than to flip Tyler over, right there on the cab seat, and use him until his own need was satisfied.

The man was nearly upon them. Though Clint knew the added dash of danger that they might be witnessed had contributed to the intensity of the little scene they'd just played out, he would never knowingly subject his sub to danger of any kind. Forcing down his raw lust, he cleared his throat. "Better rope that stallion back into the corral, boy. We got company."

Chapter 4

By the time they arrived at Lucky Harding's place, the sky had opened, the fat, heavy clouds giving up their loads with cracking thunder and streaks of lightning against the gunmetal sky.

After a dash from the truck to the front door, Clint and Tyler stood on the ranch house porch, waiting for the door to open. Though it was only going on five o'clock, the sky was dark, vividly illuminated by a flash of lightning that preceded a rejoining boom of thunder.

Clint had told Tyler he'd met Lucky Harding over the years at various state fairs and bull breeding events. The Harding Ranch was regarded as one of the premier breeders in West Texas, on par with the Ransom Ranch.

"They're like us, with prize semen that's a whole lot more valuable than the stuff Blake lost. I was hopin' to get a look around the place and see if we can't come up with some clues. But ain't no way we're goin' to do any investigatin' in this downpour."

The door finally opened, a small, plump woman with silver hair pulled back in a bun and rosy cheeks smiling up in confusion at them. "Can I help you boys?" Behind her they could hear shouts and laughter of children and the thumping of feet.

"Ma'am, I'm Clint Darrow, from the Ransom Ranch, and this is my friend, Tyler Sutton." He waved his dripping cowboy hat toward Tyler. "I spoke with Lucky this mornin' about stoppin' by. You must be Mrs.

Harding?"

The woman nodded. "Please, call me Mabel. Lucky did mention that phone call but I guess he forgot all about it." She peered up at Clint. "You're the cowboy poet, ain't that right? I saw you last year at the rodeo. You got a right pretty way of spinnin' words."

"Thank you, ma'am. Much obliged for the compliment." Clint ducked his head modestly. "Did Lucky happen to mention anything about some missin' bull semen tanks?"

"He sure did. He said a number of places have been hit in the area." She shook her head. "Ain't it a shame what the world's comin' to? We never had anything like this happen before. I can't imagine who would have done such a thing." She clucked disapprovingly, then added. "I'm right sorry, Clint, but Lucky's not here right now. He and the boys decided to get an early start, before the bad weather hit. They went to pick up a prize bull across the border. He won't be back till morning."

There were sudden childish shrieks behind Mabel, and the sound of china crashing to the ground. She spun around, crying, "Jacob Aaron, Brendan Robert! What's got into you boys? Sit down at the table right this second before I tan both your hides." The sound of a baby wailing somewhere in the distance added to the cacophony.

She turned back toward the men, her expression harried and apologetic. "Come on in out of the rain," she said. "I got my hands full with my grandkids—they're visitin' for the week and between you, me and the wall, I've had about all I can take." There was another crash and the woman hurried away, calling behind her that she'd be right back.

Clint turned to Tyler. "Oh well," he grinned. "Guess we'll have to head on into town and see if we can't find a place to stay for the night. Nothin' we could do around here today anyway, not in this weather. That suit you?"

Clint's gaze moved over him, raking his body as if Tyler were buck naked in front of him, the look in his eyes that of a hungry wolf. Tyler's cock responded and he half-turned away, willing his erection to subside before Mabel returned to the front hall.

She came back a moment later, holding a fat baby on her hip. The child's face was still tear-streaked, though she seemed content enough for the moment, sucking loudly on a pacifier, her dimpled fingers curled tight around a bit of pink blanket.

Just then a peal of thunder cracked so close the house actually shook. The baby's eyes opened in startled surprised, the pacifier falling from her mouth as she began to howl. Tyler bent and retrieved the pacifier, wiping it on his jeans before handing it to the grandmother, who gave it another wipe on her apron before trying to reinsert it into the crying child's mouth. The baby twisted her head away, her face scrunched and reddening.

"It's mine! Gimme it!"

"No it's not! I had it first!" Two small boys tumbled into view, both holding tight to a metal toy tractor painted bright green. The baby continued to cry with a piercing wail, and their grandmother looked as if she might start bawling herself.

To Tyler's surprise, Clint held out his arms. "You take care of the boys, Mabel," he said calmly. "I'll see to the baby." With a helpless look of gratitude, she handed the squalling bundle over.

Clint put the infant against his chest, her wet cheek resting on his shoulder. He began to rock on the balls of his feet, crooning a quiet lullaby in his raspy whiskey voice. To Tyler's surprise the baby quieted almost at once, relaxing her rigid little form in Clint's strong arms.

Once Mabel had seen to the boys, and they were settled in another room, she returned and stood watching Clint, her hands on her hips. "Well, I declare. You have a way with you, Mr. Darrow. You got children of your own?"

"No ma'am," Clint said. "But I'm right partial to young 'uns." The baby had fallen asleep in his arms. He continued to rock her gently and the easy tenderness with which he held her moved something deep inside Tyler.

Mabel held up her hands as if in prayer. "Would you mind terribly layin' her in her crib? I'm afraid we might wake her if we switch hands. I haven't had a moment's peace all day."

Clint nodded, smiling. "Lead the way."

He followed the woman out of the hall. Tyler stayed behind, twisting his hat in his hands as he waited. He could see into the sitting room beyond. The house reminded him of his parents' house, over-furnished in a country way, complete with an oxen yoke over the doorway and braided rag rugs scattered on the floors. He saw that the chairs were black-and-white spotted armchairs, probably covered with actual cowhide, and there were reproductions of famous cowboy paintings on the walls. A sudden intense longing for home washed over him. He'd left in the heat of anger, hounded by his own shame. Was there ever any going back?

Clint and Mabel returned a few minutes later. "Thanks ever so much," she said, smiling at Clint. Thunder rumbled and then roared and they tensed, listening for the baby's cry, but all remained quiet, other than the sound of the TV in the next room, where Mr. Rogers was exhorting the children to be his neighbor.

The rain was falling hard with no signs of letting up. "I do hope you didn't make the trip all the way out here in this weather just to see Lucky. I'm really sorry he couldn't be here, but I do expect them back bright and early tomorrow morning."

"No trouble at all," Clint replied. "We're makin' a circuit of some of the ranches and farms affected in the area. We were headed this way in any event. Now we'll get out of your hair. Would you by chance know of a motel in town?"

"I wish I could offer you accommodations here," she answered, her face falling. "But with the kids and all, there just isn't room."

"It's no problem," Clint began, but she interrupted him, her face brightening.

"I know!" she cried. "Y'all can stay in the bunkhouse. That's where Pete and Jim, our live-in ranch hands, stay, but they've gone with Lucky. There's a spare bunk with two beds. It's not luxury accommodations, but it's warm and dry, and Prancer and Gracie can keep you company."

"Horses," Tyler said, understanding at once, though it seemed to take Clint a moment to catch her meaning.

"That's right. Gracie gets a little spooked from thunder. You can give her a carrot if you want. There's a basket of them right inside the stable, which is just off the tack room from the bunkhouse."

"That's mighty nice of you, Mabel," Clint said, ducking his head toward her in appreciation. "That suit you, Tyler?"

Tyler nodded, his heart jumping at the thought of spending another night alone with Clint.

"It's right down the drive a ways," Mabel continued. "I'll turn on the floodlights. You can drive your truck down since it's raining. Do you have dry things to change into?"

They assured her they did, and, once she'd pressed fresh sheets and blankets, ham sandwiches, apples, cookies and a thermos of coffee on them and they'd offered their sincere thanks and good nights, they made their dash to the truck.

The bunkhouse was a long, rectangular room with whitewashed walls and wide-planked pinewood floors. There were two freestanding beds neatly made with patchwork quilts on them and a table set beneath a window against one wall. In one corner was a kitchen, complete with a stove, sink and small refrigerator. There was a screened-off area beside it that Tyler presumed was the bathroom. Along the far wall sat an unused bunk bed with narrow twin mattresses that presumably Mabel Harding had meant for them to use.

Tyler looked doubtfully at them and turned to Clint with a grin. "You want top or bottom bunk?"

Clint swept Tyler with another of those dark, dangerous gazes that set his innards to melting. "I got a better idea. How 'bout let's put these mattresses on the floor? Give us more space."

Tyler grinned. "Works for me."

Clint dropped his wet hat onto the table and reached for Tyler, pulling him into his arms. He kissed him hard, holding Tyler's face in his hands as he hungrily explored Tyler's mouth with his tongue. Tyler responded in kind, drinking in Clint's kisses as if he were dying of thirst.

"I've been waitin' all afternoon to do that," Clint said, when he finally let Tyler go. "And now we got all night, just you and me, boy. Just you and me." There was a fire in Clint's dark eyes that made Tyler look away, lest he tumble headlong into it and be burned to smithereens.

Ever since Clint had made him come in the truck several hours before, Tyler's mind had been going at full throttle, coming up with a thousand reasons why he needed to nip this in the bud, even while his body ached for a repeat performance.

After the whole mess with Wayne, Tyler had promised himself never again. Never again would he allow himself to be so vulnerable with another man. Never again would he hand over the reins of his desire to someone else.

And yet...

And yet since the moment he'd laid eyes on Clint Darrow, something that had been playing possum inside him these past months had leaped wide awake, eager, even desperate, to rekindle the flames he'd tried so hard to douse.

Tyler stood trying to catch his breath, his heart thrumming, his skin actually tingling with the need for Clint's touch. Though he couldn't deny his physical attraction to the cowboy, whatever was happening between them wasn't right. He had to get control of himself. He was his own man.

The rain continued to fall and a sharp crack of thunder was followed by a soft, restless whinny coming from somewhere beyond the kitchen door. Tyler headed toward it, glad for a reason to get away.

The door opened onto a tack room, the warm smells of saddle leather and damp straw causing a sudden, sharp pain of longing for his own horse, left behind at the Double S. Beyond the room were the stables, and, as promised, a basket of carrots stood at the ready.

Taking two, Tyler headed toward the horses, one with a mahogany coat and black mane who stood regal as a king. Tyler offered the dark horse a carrot, which he accepted as his due. The other, a dappled gray, was pawing the ground nervously and tossing her mane, her large eyes rolling.

"Hey there," Tyler said softly. "You must be Gracie." He moved slowly toward her, his voice low and soft. "I know how you feel, Gracie. It's scary sometimes, the things we don't understand. But it's just thunder. Clouds bumping. Nothing to be afraid of here all cozy in this nice dry stable." He reached toward her with a gentle hand, lightly touching her forehead with his finger, which he moved in a slow, easy circle. Gracie lowered her head, snuffling softly as she accepted the offered carrot.

"That's true, what you said." Tyler heard Clint behind him but didn't turn around. He continued to stroke the horse's velvet-soft head. "It's scary sometimes, the things we don't understand."

Tyler didn't reply. Clint continued. "Us cowboys, we grow up with this code, pounded into us from the moment we're born. You gotta be tough. To be vulnerable, to need another person, is seen to be weak, and no self-respectin' cowboy wants to be seen as weak. The way I see it, you and me, we was born with the deck stacked against us, seein' as we're already what you might call sexual outlaws—hankerin' after our own kind instead of the opposite sex. For you it's even tougher, at least on the surface, than for me. Because you've got this desire—this need—to submit to another person and to belong to him deeper than most folks will ever understand."

"I don't—" Tyler whirled toward Clint, ready to protest, but Clint silenced him with a hand and a word.

"Hush. Hear me out, Ty. Just listen for a little while, then you can tell me all the reasons I'm wrong."

Tyler turned back toward Gracie, who nuzzled her soft nose against his hand. Fine. He'd let Clint talk, then he'd set him straight.

"I've been payin' attention, Tyler. I know what makes you hot. I know what you need, maybe even better than you do at this point. But I also understand that it ain't somethin' that comes easy for a strong man.

"I think maybe you got the notion that what attracts you somehow makes you somethin' less than a man. The power you have in the situation is in your willingness to trust yourself, along with your judgment of the man you choose to give yourself to."

Tyler turned toward him. "Those are fine words, but I've been down this path before. I thought it was what I wanted—what I," he hesitated, stumbling over the word, "…needed, but I was just fooling myself."

He crossed his arms over his chest, refusing to let that whole horrible mess come washing back over him like a mudslide. "Something's twisted inside me—something that yearns to be used rough and taken hard. But that doesn't mean a man has the right to humiliate me or take what isn't freely given."

Clint stepped behind him, and his strong arms encircled Tyler. Clint rested his head lightly against Tyler's back. "You been hurt, Tyler. Sounds to me like some kind of bully got ahold of you and took advantage of your nature. I'm right sorry that happened to you, but it's got nothin' to do with what you and me are sharin' right now. You ain't twisted and there's nothin' wrong with you. Let go of whatever shame it is you're holdin' onto. Shame's like a rock, Ty. It weighs you down. Toss it away now—you don't need it no more. Not with me."

Clint lifted his head and kissed the back of Tyler's neck, causing all kinds of mixed emotions to course through him. "As for me," Clint continued. "I don't hold much truck with any kind of disrespect. For me it ain't about one person usin' the other, or takin' what he wants 'cause he can. It's about connection. It's about trust. And trust can't be demanded. It's got to be earned."

Clint pulled Tyler toward him. "Now come on, the rain's let up and Gracie's fine. Come on back with me to the bunkhouse and I'll show you what I mean. If you can trust me, Tyler, I can help you get back that spark I know still burns inside you. I've got a single tail whip that will show you more than a thousand words could tell you."

Tyler followed Clint back into the bunkhouse, his mind still rebelling, but his body ready, willing and eager. A single tail whip! Unbidden, unwelcome, the memory of Wayne with the riding quirt in his hand as he held Tyler against the wall, his pants around his knees, burst into Tyler's mind. He'd nearly come just from the feel of the stinging leather raining over his body, something which had confused and upset him at the time.

How humiliated he'd been when, after the whipping, Wayne had jerked him around and pushed him to his knees. He'd nearly come from that whipping, but as usual Wayne had stopped too soon, too intent on having Tyler suck him off to pay attention to Tyler's reactions.

Wayne used the whip to control Tyler. He got off on the power he could exert over Tyler. It made him feel superior. There was none of the poetry and connection Clint had hinted about. None of the passion and sweetness they'd shared the night before.

Clint moved toward the duffel bag he'd dropped to the floor when they'd entered the bunkhouse. He lifted it to the table and unzipped it, drawing out a long, coiled black whip with a short braided handle. Tyler stared at it, unable to deny the thrill just the sight of the whip produced deep in his gut. Maybe this time it would be different. *Don't be a fool*, a voice of caution whispered inside him, but he was too excited to listen.

"You have experience with a single tail, Ty?" Clint's voice was low and seductive.

"Yeah." Tyler was unable to look away from the long, supple strand of soft leather.

Clint pulled out one of the chairs from the table and settled himself onto it, stretching out his long legs and letting the whip dangle to the floor between them. "It ain't so much about the pain, is it, Ty? It's about getting past the pain. Or no, maybe a better way to say it is, it's about connecting with the pain. Harnessing it, bringing it under control, same as a wild horse, so that it gives you a power you never dreamed of before. The thing of it is, you can't get there alone. We go together, and when the connection is right, it's as intense and powerful for the one usin' the whip as it is for the one takin' it. I'll be right there with you, every step of the way."

These words startled Tyler, so different from what Wayne used to tell him: *You're mine, boy. You're a piece of ass to be used for my pleasure. I own you. I own your orgasms, I own your pain, you belong to me, and don't you forget it.* The words had never felt quite right, but Tyler hadn't argued, too desperate for the experience to question Wayne's words. Wayne was into power solely for its sake. Clint, it seemed, was more focused on what Tyler would get out of this. The notion confused him—at odds with what he thought he knew of men like this.

"You want what I'm offerin'?" Clint asked softly.

Tyler did. More than anything. Clint wasn't Wayne, and Tyler himself wasn't the man he'd been back then. Maybe Clint was right. Maybe it was time to trust—both Clint and himself.

Clint was watching him, all the while stroking the long leather whip with a lover's caress.

Without being asked, Tyler found himself pulling at his shirt and belt buckle, unzipping his jeans, kicking off his boots. Drawn by Clint's unspoken command, Tyler moved to stand in front of him. He was nervous as a long-tailed cat in a room full of rocking chairs, but his cock didn't seem to notice, pointing straight toward Clint like a divining rod.

"How you want it, Ty? You want to be on your knees? Standin'?" Clint looked up at the ceiling. A long, thick horizontal wooden beam stretched its length across the room. "Maybe a little rope to put you in the proper frame of mind?"

Wayne had never asked. In a way that had been easier, if less satisfying. But maybe it wasn't just about easy. "I want…" Tyler began, then faltered. Why was this so hard? He tried again. "I'd like…to be tied. The feeling of the rope…arms overhead…" Again he trailed off, pleading with his eyes for Clint to understand what he barely understood himself.

Clint nodded. He stood and moved toward the duffel bag, from which he extracted the rope he'd used the night before. He took Tyler's hands in his and lifted his arms overhead. "Stay that way for me," he ordered softly. He looped one end of the rope around one of Tyler's wrists and then gave the other end an expert toss over the top of the beam. This he used to tie Tyler's second wrist, pulling it taut until Tyler was forced nearly on tiptoe.

Tyler was electrified with the thrill of being bound and nearly suspended, naked and at another man's mercy. His rational mind scolded him—he'd spent all of two days with this man—could he really trust him? But his gut knew the answer, and he relaxed a little.

Clint offered a low, appreciative whistle. "What a right pretty sight." He licked his lips and grinned, but something in Tyler's expression must have given him pause, because the smile fell away from his face.

He moved close, pressing his palms gently but firmly against Tyler's chest. "This is for you, Tyler. You set the pace tonight. Every step of the way." Clint stepped behind him and let the whip's lash dangle down over Tyler's shoulder to his chest as he leaned heavily against him. A shudder moved its way through Tyler's body, part lust, part fear.

"You want this, don't you, boy? This is what your body craves, even if your mind ain't quite caught up yet," Clint murmured, his lips brushing Tyler's ear.

"I never had it...that is, when I've been whipped, it wasn't...enough. I mean, it was good but it never was...enough. I was always left...wanting, somehow. I know I'm not making any sense."

Clint moved to stand in front of him, taking Tyler's face in his hands. He kissed him gently on the lips. "You're makin' perfect sense, and I understand. This time you're gonna get all you want, Tyler. And all you need. I promise."

Clint's eyes were glittering. "We'll start nice and easy. If you want more or you need me to slow down or even stop, you tell me that, okay? Think of it like a dance, and we're learnin' the steps together. Forget whatever it was that went on before. That ain't about us. We're startin' fresh. Both of us."

An explosion of hope moved through him. That elusive experience he could never quite articulate but had always craved seemed to be waiting, offered like a promise, like a prayer. If only he could find the courage to reach for it.

"We'll work our way up nice and slow," Clint said as he massaged Tyler's shoulders. "Get a sense of your pain threshold. Your job is to focus. To take what I'm givin' you and use it to get where you need to go. It's a journey, Ty. One we'll take together, you and me. You got any questions before we start?"

"What if...?" Tyler hesitated, then shook his head, pressing his lips together.

"Go on. Speak your mind. I need to hear what you got to say." Clint ran the length of the whip along Tyler's torso and stroked its tip along Tyler's erect cock.

Tyler licked his lips. "What if I want too much? "What if it's too much for you?"

"It won't be, Ty. Because we're doin' this together. You and me, movin' in a circle, the exchange of power just as intense on my side as it is on yours. I give, you take, and by your reactions, you give back again. If it's too much, we'll both know it. I promise. You're safe here with me, Tyler. This whip isn't intended to cut the skin, or to cause you pain for its sake. This isn't an endurance test. It's a way to connect.

"It's about trust. It's about transcendin' the pain to find a higher plain. I know this sounds poetical and lofty, but trust me, there's nothin' more powerful on this earth than the experience we can find together, if we trust each other enough to take hold of it."

He kissed Tyler again, a brushing of his lips as he stroked Tyler's cock with a sure hand. Tyler, unable to help himself, leaned into the hand with a groan. Clint dropped his cock and took a step back. "You ready, boy?"

"Yeah," Tyler breathed, flexing his wrists against the ropes, his cock straining above tight balls. With a flick of his wrist, Clint snapped the single tail in the air with a sonic crack that made Tyler wince and draw in an excited breath.

Clint ran his hand down Tyler's torso. "I want you to know, I'm honored by your trust. I want to please you as much as you want to serve me. You're in good hands. Now, close your eyes and surrender to the sensations. Show me your strength and your courage. Do it for me, but more importantly, do it for yourself."

Though his heart was racing, Tyler desperately wanted what Clint was offering. He closed his eyes and took a deep breath, which he exhaled slowly, willing himself to be calm.

The first flick of the tail caressed Tyler's hip, as gentle as a lover's tongue. He opened his eyes, realizing he'd been tensing with the expectation of sharp and sudden pain. Clint moved his arm, just a slight flick of the wrist, and the tip of the tail again brushed his skin on the opposite hip, more stroke than sting.

Clint moved behind him and Tyler tensed, expecting the worst, but the leather merely kissed his skin, though with a little more urgency than before. "Slow your breathin'," he heard Clint say from behind him. "Deep and easy...that's it. You're doin' good."

This time the whip cracked and before Tyler had time to flinch, the lash struck his ass, burning a line of fire over his skin. "Yes," Tyler cried, the word pulled from his lips by the sudden bliss of pain. Again the whip struck, a parallel line stinging its way just above the first.

Tyler danced on the balls of his feet as he absorbed the erotic pain. Clint struck him a third time, just below the first stroke. "That's it. You're almost there," he said encouragingly. "You're doin' great. You have no idea how hot you look standin' there with your arms overhead, your muscles workin', strainin' and sweatin' for me." He ran his hands over Tyler's stinging ass, lightly cupping the cheeks as he leaned into him.

"Here's a confession for you," Clint went on. "I wanted you from the moment I laid eyes on you. I wanted you bad. And now, watchin' you submit so bravely to the whip, I want you even more."

Tyler leaned back into Clint's arms, thrilled and pleased that he was turning Clint on. Clint ran light fingers along Tyler's sides and he shivered from the touch. When Clint reached around to stroke his cock, he nearly came on the spot, but forced himself to hold out, as he didn't want to stop the action.

"You ready for more, Ty?"

"Yes, please," Tyler whispered, excited by the idea of submission as an act of courage, instead of laced with shame. Clint's fingers moved lightly over the welted skin.

"Fantastic," Clint breathed. "We're gonna step it up, now. Stay with me—stay focused." He stepped to the side, snapping the tip of the whip over various parts of Tyler's naked body in shockwaves of stinging pain that almost immediately transmuted into a fierce, wild pleasure. He opened his eyes and was at once mesmerized by what he saw. The whip was like an extension of Clint's powerful forearm, a snake lunging at lightning speed toward its prey.

Clint moved in slow, graceful circles around Tyler, snapping the black leather, which curled and licked at Tyler's flesh until he was trembling, his body covered in a sheen of sweat, his heart beating a mile a minute.

When Clint aimed the whip so it caught Tyler squarely across his nipple, Tyler cried out, dancing backward despite his intention to stay still. In quick succession, Clint caught the second nipple with a fiery bite of leather.

"Oh, god, oh Jesus, oh…" Tyler was teetering on the edge of something dangerous and wonderful, more powerful than he'd imagined. At that moment he wanted nothing more than to hold Clint, to taste him, to somehow convey the gratitude and love that welled inside him. His body and his soul were on fire, a bright, blissful fire lit by the sexy cowboy standing in front of him.

Clint continued to flick the whip, letting the lash curl around Tyler to stroke his ass with its fiery kiss. "Please, oh god, please...yes...please..." Tyler knew he was babbling, but he couldn't stop. "I need you. Oh, Clint, I gotta have you. I want you in my mouth. I want to worship your cock. Please..."

Clint dropped the whip and pulled Tyler into his arms. "Come here lover." With a few deft movements, Tyler's hands were free, and he brought his arms around Clint, whose rough, calloused fingers were moving over his body, soothing the skin he'd struck a moment before.

Tyler couldn't remember feeling more aroused in his entire life, or more...grateful. Still trembling, he sank to his knees. With shaking fingers, he tugged at Clint's belt buckle and pulled at the buttons of his jeans. Clint didn't stop him, nor did he help. He put his hands on Tyler's shoulders, staring down at him with that wolfish smile.

Tyler pulled at Clint's underwear and Clint's cock sprang free, erect and dripping. Hungrily, Tyler closed his mouth over its girth, taking it in as deep as he could before sliding back, his tongue dancing along the smooth, taut flesh.

He sucked with abandon, as if he could take the whole of Clint into himself, as if they could become one person. Lust, gratitude and a curious, powerful joy threatened to overwhelm his senses. He forced himself to focus on pleasing the man standing before him, aware of his own cock rubbing against Clint's denim-clad leg with each deep-throated kiss.

It wasn't long before Clint was coming, shuddering and arching against Tyler, his hand on the back of Tyler's head as he climaxed. Tyler sucked and licked, eagerly swallowing Clint's seed. He turned his head so his cheek rested against Clint's bared thighs, his heart beating in time to the throb in his cock.

Clint reached down, stroking Tyler's hair, pushing the matted, sweat-soaked bangs from his forehead. Tyler could have stayed there forever, his arms around this remarkable man. He felt a tenderness that was new to him, especially in the context of the kind of sex he had just shared with Clint. When Wayne had used him and roughed him up a bit, Tyler had been exhilarated, frightened, even thrilled. He'd been grateful for whatever Wayne cared to toss his way, while also deeply ashamed that he craved it so bad. But this was different, so different. He looked up at Clint, making sure he was really there, and not just some much longed-for dream.

"My, oh my," Clint said, looking down at him with a smile. "That was amazin', boy. Now it's your turn. I want to make you come."

"Uh, looks like we might be a little late." Embarrassed, Tyler looked down at his gooey cock and back up at Clint with a sheepish smile. "Sorry about your boots, Sir."

"Not to worry, Ty," Clint laughed. "You'll be lickin' 'em clean."

Chapter 5

"This here's where we keep our tanks." Lucky Harding, a tall man with a bald head and a long, drooping gray mustache, led Clint and Tyler into a small building off the main barn. The door was padlocked, and they waited while he dug into his pocket for the key.

Clint and Tyler had awoken early, setting the mattresses back in their frames and taking turns in the tiny shower stall before heading into town for breakfast. Upon their return to Harding's ranch, they'd been greeted by the owner, who apologized for being absent the day before. They exchanged the requisite small talk before getting down to the heart of their visit.

"I can't believe the day's come where I got to lock stuff up, but that's the modern world for you." Lucky frowned and shrugged as he opened the padlock. He moved toward the large sturdy metal shelves where several rows of semen tanks stood. He pointed to a medium-sized tank labeled *Mama's Boy*. "This one here's worth quite a pretty penny. That bull's sperm has impregnated half the cows this side of Abilene. We sell in New Mexico and Colorado too." Lucky patted the canister with a look of satisfaction.

"We had a tank go missin' too, with prize quality semen, same as Mama's Boy there." Clint nodded toward the shelf. "The odd thing of it is, we keep a watchful eye back at our place. Ain't no one comin' or goin' that we don't recognize on sight. How about you? You had any strangers millin' about the place? Anything unusual you can pinpoint during the time your tanks disappeared?"

Lucky scratched his head, lost in thought. "Nope. Can't think of a single stranger. It ain't like folks just wander in. We're not exactly on the beaten path. That's the mystery of it."

Clint nodded, thoughtful. Tyler said, "Can you tell us exactly who came and went on the day and maybe the days leading up to when you realized the tanks were gone?" He held his pad at the ready. Clint nodded, figuring that was as good a place to start as any.

"Let's see," Lucky said, again scratching his bald pate as if this helped to jumpstart his brain. "There was Frank Corsair, deliverin' the hay. And Hoss Johnson and his boy were by earlier. In fact, that's when we figured out we was missin' some—Hoss prefers Buffalo Bill's seed—cheap but gets the job done."

He grinned, and then pursed his mouth in concentration. "Oh, and Doc Crawford came by for his regular visit. He brought out the big truck for the annual exams. Got all that fancy equipment nowadays. Must have cost him a fortune, but I imagine we'll all be payin' for it, one way or the other. Don't nothin' come cheap anymore."

That sparked something in Clint's mind. "Now that you mention it, the vet was supposed to be out at our place around the time the tank went missin'. I was away on ranch business, though, so I can't be sure."

"Ah ha." Tyler scribbled on his pad. "We have a clue. The vet was here and he was at the Ransom Ranch. And didn't Seth Blake mention that's when he discovered his missing tank? When the vet was out to check on his cow? I think we may have found our connection."

Lucky laughed, shaking his head. "Hank Crawford is the kind of guy you'd trust with your babies. Or your prize bulls, for that matter."

Clint nodded his agreement. "Yeah. Doc Crawford would never stoop to stealin' bull semen. Besides, he's been a fixture in these parts nigh on twenty years."

They talked about other possible leads, including a group of ruffian teenagers Lucky had noticed in town loitering around the country store, looking like they were up to no good. "Sometimes these kids just go on a stealing spree, for no other reason than to show off for each other. They probably didn't even know what they were takin'."

"That might hold water if yours was the only incident, Lucky. But we've got at least four places been hit over the past month, and over the whole dang county. And that's just the ones we know about. No, it's somethin' more organized."

"Well, it don't make sense," Lucky said. "Who would buy stolen semen? It's all documented. They wouldn't be able to sell it for anything like its actual worth. What's the point of takin' it?"

"That's what I aim to find out," Clint said. "I hope once we make the rounds of the other farms and ranches affected, we'll get more clues and start puttin' the pieces together. Whatever's goin' on, we got to stop it. We can't wait on the local authorities to take their sweet ass time."

Any trace of the thunderstorm the day before was long gone, the air hot and arid, and getting hotter by the minute. "A real scorcher today," Lucky noted, wiping his gleaming dome with a kerchief. "Summer's in full swing, that's for sure."

"Yeah. I guess we ought to head on. We're going to stop by Hoss Johnson's place. I'll keep you posted if we figure this thing out. Meanwhile, keep those padlocks in place. Can't be too careful these days," Clint said.

"Amen to that," Lucky agreed.

~*~

The truck bounced over the rutted road as they headed toward the

Johnson farm. Clint tried his cell phone and got a signal. He placed a call to Hoss Johnson, but it went to voicemail. He left a message asking if they could swing by, and to please give him a call at his earliest convenience.

It was hot in the truck and the air conditioner, while doing its best, just wasn't up to the task of cooling the hundred degree air that day. He'd replenished the Dr. Pepper supply, and reached now for a cold one, his hand brushing Tyler's thigh as he opened the cooler.

"Boy, it sure is hot," Tyler said.

"Yeah. This old truck's 'bout had it," Clint agreed. He cranked down the windows and Tyler reached for the radio. Merle Haggard's distinctive, gruff voice filled the cab.

"Good ol' Merle," Tyler said, surprising Clint that he knew the old-time artist. Merle was singing about being an Okie from Muskogee. Tyler chimed in on the line about white lightning.

Something eased inside him. True, they were only nine years apart, but that was enough of a gap to include a whole generation.

Another song came on the radio, the man's voice rich and powerful, the soulful guitar licking beneath his words like a lover's kiss. The man singing warned his lover to keep their distance, that they must give all or none at all.

"That's Richard Thompson," Tyler announced, further impressing Clint. "I saw him live in Austin. He's amazing."

"Can't say as I know him," Clint said. "But I like the sound of this music. It's mournful but with a kind of hope, if you know what I mean." Tyler nodded and Clint felt he really did know. They rode on in companionable silence for a while, listening to the radio and drinking their soda.

When they were only a few miles from Hoss Johnson's place, Clint tried again to reach him on his cell, but had no luck. The back of his shirt was soaked and sticking to the leather of the seat. He turned apologetically to Tyler, whose blond hair had darkened with sweat, his fair cheeks flushed from the heat. "Guess we should have taken your fancy car, huh? Sorry about that. This heat spell came on pretty sudden."

Tyler shrugged. "It's okay. I'm no stranger to West Texas summers."

Taking this as a lead-in, Clint ventured, "You wanna talk about it some, Ty? Why you really left the ranch? What happened to make you so gun shy?"

Tyler wiped his forehead with the back of his shirt sleeve, pushing a wing of damp hair away, though it promptly fell back again. "I'm too hot to talk about anything." Tyler looked out his window so Clint could no longer see his face.

Clint nodded, accepting that for the time being. After all, despite the intensity of their experience so far, they really barely knew one another. And in fairness, he'd told Tyler next to nothing about himself.

Sensing he had to give Tyler room, he kept his tone light. Now wasn't the time to speak of things that mattered. He forced himself to focus on their mission. After all, his boss had given him a specific task—to find out what had happened to their tanks and, if possible, to get them back.

If only Hoss would call back. He drummed his fingers a moment on the steering wheel as he marshaled his thoughts. He stared at the cell phone on the seat beside him, willing it to ring.

"It's too hot to wait in the truck," Clint said, turning to Tyler, "but I don't want to go on without checkin' out Johnson's place. I got an idea. If memory serves, there's a creek off the road not too far from here. We could take a swim and cool off. I got towels and stuff in the back of the truck. How's that sound?"

"Sounds great," Tyler said, turning back to him with a smile.

Clint maneuvered the truck onto a narrow rutted dirt road that paralleled a thicket of trees. He drove alongside it a while until he found a break in the trees. Turning the wheel, he drove through the brush, following the sound of the water, now an audible rush and tumble in the quiet.

Past the thicket the creek appeared, the water frothing and sparkling in the sunlight, surely as inviting as any oasis in the desert to the hot, sweat-soaked men. Clint pulled up alongside the creek and switched off the engine. The place was just as he'd remembered it.

"How'd you find this place?" Tyler asked, as they climbed out of the truck.

"Friend of mine used to be from around here. Fellow by the name of Lee Spencer."

"Used to be? As in past tense?"

"Well, he's still a friend, but back when we first met I was wet behind the ears, maybe twenty or so." He pulled up the tarp that covered the truck bed and rummaged for the bag where he kept spare towels and blankets. "I was still explorin' back then. Figurin' out who I was."

"Meaning if you were gay or not?" Tyler asked.

"Nah, I knew that since I was in grammar school." He paused, adding, "Remember that show, *Bonanza*?"

"I've seen it on cable a few times."

"Well, I had a powerful hankerin' for Adam Cartwright. You know, the oldest son who always wore black." Tyler nodded. "When I was about twelve and discovered masturbation, he was who I thought about. I imagined he would ride up to my family's farm late at night and steal me away. He'd keep me holed up at his cabin somewhere in the mountains, his captive sex slave, forced to do all sorts of unspeakable acts."

Clint grinned at the memory, shaking his head. How lonely he'd been as a boy, never telling a soul who or what he really was. His father, an old-fashioned West Texas, God fearing Baptist, would have whipped him within an inch of his life if he'd ever had an inkling his boy was a queer.

"You imagined yourself as a sex slave?" Tyler looked confused. "But you're the one who likes being in control."

"I am now. Back then I was findin' my way. My first sexual experiences were an exploration. I didn't know what I was, to tell you the truth. It was Lee who showed me how powerful this kind of lovin' can be. He taught me a lot."

"So you started out like me?" Tyler still looked perplexed.

Clint nodded. "When you're first gettin' involved in that stuff, you got no clue what you're doin'. It's natural to gravitate to someone who does—someone who wants to teach." Clint handed Tyler the bundle of towels and blankets, and returned to the truck cab to retrieve the cooler.

"The idea of sex, power and pain always fascinated me," he continued, as they walked toward the creek. "At first I explored it from a different side, I guess you could say. Took me some time to figure out what I was and what I needed."

Tyler seemed to ponder this. Then he asked, "So what happened to Lee? You said you're still friends…"

"Yeah. He hooked up with a guy who lives in Fort Worth.

Occasionally I get out that way and we get together for a beer or what have you. He taught me a lot, and I'll always be grateful for the lessons. He respected my limits and never took me further than I was ready to go. It's one reason I'm comfortable today with who I am. You see, everythin' I ask of you, Ty, I've done myself."

"You don't say…" Tyler seemed genuinely puzzled by this, making Clint wonder anew just what his previous experience had been.

They set up the blanket beside the creek, which looked very inviting, the water clear as it rushed over smooth pebbles on the sandy bottom. They stripped to their underwear. Tyler looked around. "You sure this is safe? Nobody's gonna suddenly show up with their picnic baskets and kids?"

Clint shook his head. "Nah, no one ever did when Lee and I used to come here. There's a lake not too far from here with a nice sandy shore. That's where folks with families go. I reckon we got the place all to ourselves."

"All right then," Tyler said, as he pulled his briefs down his strong, tan legs. Before Clint could finish admiring his naked form, Tyler stepped down into the creek bed, moving toward its center, which at its deepest only came up to his chest. He ducked down into the water, rising up a moment later like some kind of blond sea god, shaking his hair and spraying the surface with droplets of water that shimmered gold in the sunlight.

"Man, that's cold," he said, hugging himself. "But it feels great. You coming in?"

Clint shucked his underwear and stepped into the rushing water, moving toward Tyler. The cool water hit his hot body with a shock, but after a few seconds he'd adjusted enough to submerge his sweat-soaked head, letting the water sluice over him and wash him clean. It was colder than he remembered, but that was probably due to the rain of the day before.

He resurfaced, looking for Tyler. He felt him before he saw him, curling around his legs like a large fish before he popped up in front of Clint, laughing and spraying him with water as he shook back his hair from his face.

Clint caught him in a bear hug, happiness surging through him. He couldn't remember feeling this carefree in many a year. This had gone way beyond a simple pickup of a likeminded gay man for some casual, if intense, sex. He was falling for Tyler Sutton, though he hadn't a clue what the future held between them, if anything at all.

Tyler was a big guy, a little taller than Clint, and broader in the shoulder and torso, but in the water they were more equally weighted. On an impulse, Clint reached down, catching Tyler beneath his ass and hoisting him upward into his arms. Tyler laughed, wrapping his strong legs around Clint's waist.

Clint's cock rose in appreciation as he kissed Tyler's warm, inviting lips. He shifted, lifting Tyler higher in his arms until the head of his cock rested against Tyler's nether entrance. He would have liked nothing better than to plunge into that tight passage right there in the creek.

Tyler wriggled back against Clint's cock with a sexy sigh, lifting his legs to Clint's shoulders. The head of Clint's cock nearly slipped into him. Clint moved back. "Whoa there, Ty. You're gonna get somethin' you ain't ready for if you keep that up."

"Oh, I'm ready for it," Tyler said, his eyes narrowing as he licked his lips. "I want it, Clint. I want it bad." The way Tyler was positioned, the backs of his strong thighs resting against Clint's shoulders, his tight, muscular ass spread so Clint's cock nestled between its cheeks, was so inviting that it took every ounce of Clint's willpower not to penetrate him then and there, condoms and lubrication be damned.

Instead he ducked down in the water, pulling away so Tyler's body slid from his. They both stood again, pressing close as they reached for each other's cock beneath the cool, rushing water. They kissed as they stroked one another, panting against each other's lips as their tongues danced.

"I want you to fuck me," Tyler murmured throatily. After a beat he added, "Please, Sir."

Clint needed no further invitation. They waded back to the creek's bank and clambered out, bodies dripping, cocks at the ready. Tyler flopped down on the blanket, watching as Clint reached for the wallet from the back pocket of his jeans. He riffled through it, frowning. "Dang. I can't find what I'm lookin' for in here."

Tyler jumped up, eager as a puppy. "I got some. Pre-lubed and everything." He grabbed his jeans and jammed his hand in a pocket, tossing a small packet toward Clint, who caught it, laughing.

Once he was properly sheathed, he said, "Get on your hands and knees. Offer yourself to me, boy."

Tyler, who had been lying on his side, cocked on one elbow with his head cradled in his hand, rolled over and positioned himself as ordered. He twisted back to watch Clint as he crouched behind him. Clint entered him slowly, letting Tyler's body heat the lubricated latex so it eased inside.

"I don't want you to move," he said, as he draped his body over Tyler's strong back. "This is an exercise in discipline. No matter what I do to you, you stay stock still. Don't push back, don't try to take any control. Okay?"

Tyler nodded and Clint could actually feel his barely restrained, restless desire, like an eager stallion who, once saddled, anticipates the wild ride ahead. "Answer me, boy," Clint added. "I want to hear you."

"Yes, Sir," Tyler said, his voice thick with lust. Clint's cock surged and he felt the involuntary clutch of Tyler's muscles spasming against it. He groaned with pleasure and began to move inside.

When Tyler arched slightly back, Clint reached for his hair, which he used like a rein to jerk Tyler's head back. "I said, don't move," he reminded the boy, who gasped, his lips parting.

His fingers still entwined in Tyler's thick, wet hair, Clint moved again, shifting and sliding inside the hot, perfect grip of Tyler's body. Tyler groaned, a shudder moving through him. Clint reached for his cock, wrapping his hand around it as he fucked Tyler from behind.

It was as if he were not only inside Tyler's body, but also his very soul. He could feel Tyler's act of will, trying desperately to hold still while Clint moved inside him, all the while stroking and teasing Tyler's rock-hard shaft. Clint couldn't deny the deep, satisfying thrill he got from bending this strong, sexy man to his will. He didn't know which was better—the hot, slick clutch of Tyler's ass on his cock, or the sweet tremble of Tyler's body as he struggled to obey Clint's dictate to be still.

"Oh, god," Tyler groaned, as Clint stroked his hard cock with a sure hand as he moved inside. "I can't…Clint, I can't stay still. My body needs to…oh…" He began to shudder, his back arching, his hips thrusting back to take Clint in deep. Clint jerked Tyler's head back by the hair and Tyler twisted toward him, accepting Clint's rough, desperate kiss.

Clint felt the rushing rise of his own release as he kissed the boy, all the while pumping Tyler's cock in his fist. Tyler was no longer trying to be still, and Clint gave him a silent reprieve. They were both sweating again in the hot, dry air, their bodies slippery as they moved together, panting and grunting.

Clint was poised on the edge of orgasm, savoring the exquisite torture of holding himself back as long as he could. He finally let go when he felt the sudden warm spurt of semen over his fingers as Tyler cried out.

Clint jerked hard, the weight of his orgasm propelling him forward as they fell together to the blanket, Tyler beneath him, Clint's cock still buried deep inside. They lay still for a long time, the only movement the combined galloping of their hearts, which finally slowed in tandem to a cantor and then a walk.

After a time, Clint became aware of the jangle of his cell phone from the heap of their clothing nearby, and realized he'd been drifting in a contented, easy doze.

Tyler stretched languidly beside him. "You gonna get that?"

While Clint was considering this, the phone stopped ringing. "Guess not." He grinned and playfully smacked Tyler's bare ass. Pushing himself to his feet, he said, "Race you to the creek."

With his limp, he didn't have a chance in hell of beating the younger man, but he didn't mind. He enjoyed watching Tyler lope toward the water in all his naked glory. He joined Tyler in the water, smiling as he watched Tyler duck down and rise a moment later, shaking his wet hair and laughing. Clint found himself laughing too, just for sheer joy.

"Ain't it great," Tyler said, echoing his thoughts, "to be alive?"

Chapter 6

"It's like I told you the other night," Hoss Johnson said. "Couple of our tanks disappeared. One of them didn't even have nothin' in it. But even empty, they don't come cheap, you know."

"Was Doc Crawford here sometime around when you noticed them going missing?" Tyler tried to keep his voice neutral, feeling almost like he imagined a trial attorney might, who didn't want to lead the witness.

Hoss glanced at Tyler, but focused on Clint to answer, which mildly annoyed Tyler, but he let it pass. Hoss Johnson had no doubt labeled him a city boy not worth his time or attention. Tyler shrugged inwardly at this. He was on a story, and if this country boy preferred to deal with one of his own, that was fine by Tyler.

"Now that you mention it," he drawled, his eyes still on Clint, as if Clint had asked the question, "he *was*. Him and that new assistant of his." He looked at Tyler now and furrowed his brow suspiciously. "How'd you know that?"

"It seems to be the one consistent thread with all these thefts," Tyler said. "Every time one of these tanks go missing, the vet appears to have been on the scene."

Hoss laughed, shaking his head dismissively, as Clint and Lucky Harding had done before. "Not Doc Crawford. He's the salt of the earth. As honest as the day is long."

"New assistant," Tyler said. "What's his name? Do you know him? Has he worked for Doc Crawford long?" Tyler glanced at Clint, who shook his head and shrugged.

Hoss answered, "He's pretty new. Helps the doc with drivin' and routine checkups and vaccinations, that sort of stuff. Learnin' the ropes, I'd say. Seems like a nice enough fellow—very polite. Seems to know his stuff."

"Hmm," Clint mused. "Are you thinkin' he might be the culprit?"

"I'm just collecting information at this point," Tyler said. "Then we sift through it and see what we come up with." Turning back to Hoss, he asked, "Have you noticed anyone else around when the tanks were taken? Anything else unusual we should follow up on? Any new employees?"

"I have two new hired hands, Jake Johnson and Ronnie Gray. But I've known 'em both since they was kids. I don't hire just anybody, you know." He scowled at Tyler, as if Tyler had just accused him of something.

"Just collecting facts," Tyler reminded him. "Getting the big picture." He underlined the words *vet's assistant* on his pad, determined to follow that lead. "We should find out more about Doc Crawford's new assistant," he said to Clint.

"You think so?" Clint mused. "Texas may be big, but ranch folks is tight, and word's bound to get around. There's no way in hell he could sell that semen to anyone within a hundred mile radius. He'd be busted in ten seconds flat."

Tyler sucked at the tip of his pen, musing. "Yeah. But somebody is taking these tanks, that's a fact we can't get around. I wonder," he turned questioningly to Clint, "if there's a way we could check this guy out without tipping our hand or offending the vet. Maybe," he added, warming to the idea, "we could do a kind of stakeout. See if we couldn't catch him in the act."

"Not a bad idea," Clint said. "But how we gonna know where they go next? We can't just trail them around the whole county and show up on folks' property."

"I could call Betty Jo, Doc Crawford's receptionist, and see if she'd tell us the doc's schedule." Hoss offered. "She's my cousin."

"That might work," Clint said, nodding.

Tyler tried to keep his face neutral, but inside he was excited. These men were taking him seriously, and together they might actually solve this thing. He'd make sure the case was wrapped up tight, getting all the facts and evidence to write up a good article for the magazine. He could go into depth on the background of the case—the underlying motivations for the crime, the local color, how local law enforcement deals with situations like these... He pulled himself up short, reining in his imagination. The crime wasn't solved yet. He needed to focus on that first. They'd need solid evidence before any accusations were made.

Hoss, who'd been busy on his cell phone, flicked it shut. "You boys are in luck. The doc's makin' house calls today. He'll be headin' over to the Riley ranch this afternoon for some annual checkups. Takin' the big equipment truck *and* his new assistant with him. If you get a move on, you might make it there before he does."

"Great," Tyler enthused, excited at the idea of a stakeout. Maybe they'd catch the guy right in the act. He turned to Clint. "You know this Riley fellow, Clint? We could call ahead and make plans."

"Sure, yeah, I know him." Clint spoke in a flat voice, not meeting Tyler's eye.

"Is there a problem?" Tyler asked carefully.

Clint shrugged, still not looking directly at him. "No. No problem.

Seems like as good a plan as any."

They said their farewells to Hoss Johnson and climbed into the truck. Tyler kept waiting for Clint to offer some explanation for his sudden change in mood, but Clint remained silent, eyes on the road.

They'd been driving a full twenty minutes before Tyler, silently debating whether to press the issue, finally blurted, "What's going on?"

It took Clint a while to answer. Tyler waited and finally Clint glanced his way. "Ain't nothin' goin' on," he said, but his eyes said otherwise.

It suddenly occurred to Tyler where they were headed. Riley's ranch was a stone's throw from Clint's ranch, at least in Texas terms. Could it be Clint didn't want to be seen with him around folks he knew well? Was all that talk about being comfortable with who and what you are just so much guff when it came down to it?

He looked at Clint, who kept his face doggedly focused on the road, and his heart contracted with confusion. Damn it, he had begun to trust Clint in a way he never had another person, even though their time together had been so brief. Was this the end then? Would he return to Austin, Clint to his ranch, and that would be that?

Tyler tested the idea in his mind, trying it on. He would go back to the big, impersonal city, to the gay bars where guys without names would invite him home for an hour or a night of empty pleasure. Clint and the possibility of what he'd offered would be relegated to memories he hauled out at night until even the memories faded into half-forgotten dreams of what might have been.

This was stupid. Clint Darrow couldn't possibly do such an abrupt about-face with no rhyme or reason. Tyler forced himself to be calm. Something was troubling him, was all.

"Clint?" Tyler reached out, putting his hand on Clint's forearm "You going to talk to me? Ever since the mention of Riley's place, you went all quiet and strange. Did something happen to upset you?"

"Here's the thing," Clint said slowly, as if marshaling his thoughts. "You and I met in a kind of a vacuum, if you understand me."

"No, not really. What're you trying to say?" Tyler held his breath, not sure he wanted to hear what came next, but knowing he had to.

"Meanin' we both have lives we been livin' before we met each other. I hadn't counted on how close you and me got, and how fast. It's about more than just the sex between us. We got somethin' important happenin', at least I think we do, and now here comes real life to mess with us."

Something cold entered his stomach, making it churn. *Real life?* "Just what're you saying, Clint? Stop speaking in riddles."

Clint took a breath and blew it out. "I guess I should probably have said somethin' sooner. At the Riley ranch, there's a guy there, name of Jonas Hall. We've been, uh, friends for years."

"Friends," Tyler said, drawing out the word as his heart sank.

"Friends with benefits," Clint admitted, confirming Tyler's fears.

"And you were planning on telling me this…?" Even as Tyler said this, he knew he had no right. They'd been together, if you could even call it that, for all of three days. He had "friends" too, back in Austin, so what was the big deal?

Clint didn't answer, and Tyler tried to take him off the hook. "Hey, it's okay. I mean, you and me, we're…just friends too, I guess." Aware even as he said it that he was speaking more out of disappointment than truth, he added, "Shit, maybe not even that."

He turned away, unable suddenly to bear looking at Clint's powerful profile. At last he'd found a man who understood him—who took charge the way Tyler longed for, and it was slipping away just that fast.

Clint said nothing. After a while, Tyler shot him a sidelong glance. Clint's lips were pressed together in a thin line, his fingers gripping the steering wheel so hard his knuckles were white.

"Hey," Tyler said. "I don't know why I said that. It was stupid." Clint didn't reply. "Look," Tyler went on doggedly, feeling miserable. "Is my being there going to cause you a problem? Because I can wait in—"

"No, it's okay." Clint looked his way, his smile asking, it seemed to Tyler, forgiveness, or at least a truce. "We got a mystery to solve."

~*~

Tyler felt almost foolish, staked out behind the shed where George Riley said they kept their semen tanks. Clint had spoken with George on his cell as they drove, sketching out a plan of action for the stakeout. They'd agreed not to talk to the vet or his assistant directly, since their suspicions were as yet unfounded.

They'd decided to wait instead and see if they couldn't catch the guy in the act. Clint had gone to park his truck out of sight while Tyler hid near the shed where the semen tanks were kept, his small digital camera at the ready.

Though Tyler had wanted to talk more about their situation, he couldn't seem to get any words past the lump in his throat. Clint hadn't seemed inclined to talk about it either. The ease had somehow been drained from their relationship, and Tyler didn't know how to get it back. Could it be this Jonas guy meant more to Clint than he was letting on? Was Tyler now the third wheel, just in the way?

He should have known better than to buy all Clint's pretty lines about honesty and understanding. After all, Clint was the one who had been holding out, never once mentioning he had this "friend with benefits" waiting for him at the ranch next to his own. So much for his assertions about how important trust was in a relationship.

Relationship, my ass, Tyler thought bitterly. *What a fool I was, thinking this time would be any different.*

But it *had* been different, and he knew it. What they'd shared had been way beyond the realm of a quick fuck. It had *mattered.* Well, at least to him it had. The jury in his mind was now out on the cowboy, and it was quite possible a mistrial would be declared before they came back with a verdict.

There was the sound of an engine and then the crunch of the large wheels of the vet's equipment van as it was backed toward the shed. Tyler tensed, all thoughts of Clint momentarily flying from his head as he watched, waiting to see what, if anything, happened next.

A young man emerged from the van, walking toward the rear doors, which he opened. He appeared to be in his early twenties, if that, tall and gangly with short sandy hair and a narrow sallow face. Glancing quickly around him, he walked toward the shed.

He pulled open the doors and walked inside as if he owned the place. A moment later he emerged, hefting a rather large liquid nitrogen tank that contained who knew how much valuable bull sperm.

Tyler zoomed the digital camera lens in on the culprit and clicked a series of pictures, shooting continuously as he watched the guy load the tank into the van, slam the doors shut, and drive back toward the cow barns, which was no doubt where he'd been supposed to be heading in the first place.

Tyler's heart was beating fast. He'd caught the thief in the act, the proof now tucked away in his shirt pocket. He could follow up on the rest of the story once the authorities were called. He could enlist Clint's help in getting the background stories on the vet and the folks affected. He could delve into the thief's motivations and how he'd sold the semen, if that's what he'd done.

He could see his byline now featured prominently at the top of a two-page spread. Maybe he'd even get a teaser line on the cover: *Bull Semen Stealing Spree Stopped in its Tracks.*

As he hurried back to the main house, eager to find Clint and tell him the news, he stopped short. This investigation had been his ostensible reason for sticking around. Now that the case was solved, what would happen between them? Especially now that Clint was back on his home turf, and back with the "friend" who had put such a pall on their newfound relationship. Was this the end?

As Tyler approached, he saw George Riley talking to the vet. George looked up at Tyler's approach, a question on his face. Since it was his tank that had just been stolen in broad daylight, Tyler felt compelled to share what he'd found right away, though he wished Clint was there to witness his moment of glory. "It's what we thought. I got it all on my camera. You'll find one of your tanks in the back of Doc Crawford's equipment van."

"Oh my lord," Doc Crawford exclaimed. He appeared to be in his late sixties or early seventies, with watery blue eyes and a head of thinning white hair brushed straight back. "George was just tellin' me of your suspicions. Steve's been known to have his troubles, but I really thought he'd turned himself around this time. He hasn't missed a day of work since he started. Has a knack with the livestock too. I really thought he'd turned a corner." The vet sighed heavily. "Poor Angeline, rest her soul. I'm glad she didn't have to see this day. She always had her hands full with that boy."

He looked to Tyler. "You say you've got evidence? A stolen tank is in my van?"

Tyler produced the camera and showed the two men the pictures. George Riley called the sheriff's office and reported the theft. "They're on their way," he said. Turning to Tyler he added, "That was some good detecting work by you boys. Clint says you're a reporter for *Lone Star Monthly*, that right?"

"It is," Tyler affirmed. "And I'll be writing an article for the magazine about this whole thing. I'd like to follow up—do a full exposé, delve into his motives and how he thought he could resell the stuff without proof of its origins."

"Sheriff Oates will get it out of him, if anyone can," George said grimly.

"Oh my lord," Doc Crawford again intoned, his face etched with misery, and Tyler felt almost guilty for proving his new assistant to be a thief.

"Where's Clint?" he asked, annoyed at the tiny leap his heart took just at the mention of the cowboy's name.

"He parked his truck back at the old hay barn. Probably chewing the fat with some of the boys." George pointing toward a barn in the near distance. To the vet he said, "We better get on back to the dairy barn and see what your young Steve's doing. No telling what other mischief he's getting up to, with no one watching."

The two men hurried away. Tyler headed in the direction George had pointed. The first barn he came to looked freshly painted, with bales of hay piled just outside. Clint's truck was nowhere in sight.

Tyler walked past the barn and spied the building George must have been referring to. Clint's truck was parked in the dirt in front of an old barn with faded red sides, the paint peeling to bare wood in spots. But where was Clint?

Tyler moved toward the door, pulling it open as he called out, "Clint?" The large room was lit only by a small window, the hazy sunlight filtered through dust and grime. It took Tyler's eyes a moment to adjust to the gloom.

Two men were scuffling in the corner, grunting and breathing hard. It took a few seconds for Tyler's brain to register that one of the men was Clint, the other guy a big burly bear of a man. The man flipped Clint to ground in a sudden move and fell to his knees, straddling Clint's chest as he leaned forward.

A different scene leaped from its troubled sleeping place in Tyler's memory—Wayne pinning Tyler in the dirt, his fingers pressing hard against Tyler's larynx. Wayne had crossed a line that night, leaving bruises on Tyler's throat and fear in his gut that things had gone way too far.

The scene before him now flickered and jumped in the half-light, like the scenes on a spool of film clattering madly through a broken projector. Tyler's body jerked into action, hurtling across the space toward the men. Clint was in trouble.

He grabbed Clint's attacker, wrenching the man's thick arm back, while his other hand curled into a fist. "What the fuck you think you're doing?" he heard himself shouting, as his knuckles made contact with the man's hard jaw.

The man, still on his knees, angled sharply toward him and before Tyler could react, landed a punch on Tyler's shoulder that sent him sprawling back into the dirt. Pain shot down Tyler's arm, but he barely noticed it as he leaped to his feet, his blood boiling. The man, too, had risen.

Clint scrambled up, moving fast so he was suddenly between them, his arms held out toward either man, palms up. "Hey," he shouted. "Both of you calm down. We got a misunderstandin' goin' on." Tyler moved to the left, determined to keep his eye on the burly guy hiding behind Clint, but Clint moved too, blocking his view.

"Tyler, get a hold of yourself. I'm tellin' you everythin's fine. Ain't nobody bein' attacked here. You hear me?" Clint reached for his shoulders, which he shook until Tyler focused on him, finally hearing his words.

"We were just tusslin', Ty. Give it up." Clint released his shoulders and caught Tyler in a firm bear hug, pinning his arms to his sides in the process.

Tyler understood it all in a rush. He hadn't burst in on a fight, but on lovers locked in a playful tussle. He felt stupid and embarrassed, the feelings blurred together into something more like anger. "Well, excuse me for giving a fuck," he snapped, jerking out of Clint's embrace.

"This must be the boy you were tellin' me about," the man who Tyler knew must be Jonas Hall said in the same slow drawl that Clint favored. "I reckon he needs a few lessons in manners." He rubbed his jaw, but Tyler saw he was grinning.

"I thought you were fighting," Tyler offered, the anger sliding back down into embarrassed chagrin.

Clint nodded, a smiling lifting one side of his mouth, though he shook his head. "Understandable. Jonas and I just enjoy a little horseplay now and again. It's our way of sayin' hello. Jonas likes to try and take control from time to time, until I remind him who's really in charge."

Tyler looked toward the big man, who laughed. "Clint likes to think so, anyway." He and Clint exchanged a look of tenderness that, despite his promises to himself not to care, made Tyler's heart spasm.

"Hey, you," Clint said, again putting his strong arms around Tyler. "Everythin's okay. Like I told you on the way here, me and Jonas, we're friends. Friends with benefits, and for the way we have to live around these parts that's a special thing."

Tyler stole a glance at Jonas, who was nodding. Clint let Tyler go and stepped back. "Jonas and me go back years, and I ain't gonna apologize for his existence, or deny it. Yeah, maybe I should have told you sooner, and for that I'm sorry but that don't change the way I feel for you."

He paused a moment, collecting his thoughts while the warmth of his last words soothed Tyler. "You know," Clint continued, his voice soft but firm, "love comes in all kinds of forms and sometimes in the most unexpected places. It's a shame to turn your back on it, just 'cause you're scared or confused."

He fixed Tyler with a penetrating gaze. "That's where trust comes in. I hope you can trust me enough to get past this bit of craziness between us. You've come to mean a whole lot to me this past week, Ty. I want you in my life, and if this hasn't scared you clean away, I'd like to introduce you, proper-like this time, to my friend, Jonas Hall."

In spite of himself, a grin curled itself over Tyler's face. He'd acted like a fool, but Clint was giving him a second chance. "I ain't goin' nowhere," he said firmly, allowing himself to drift into the local vernacular that he'd purposely shed when moving to Austin.

"Well, then." Clint nodded toward Jonas. "Let's just start this whole thing over. Tyler Sutton, this here's Jonas Hall."

Jonas moved toward him, a huge hand extended. "Pleased to meet you," he said, chuckling again as he caught Tyler's hand in a strong grip. "Though I got to say, bein' sucker punched ain't exactly the most friendly greetin'." He rubbed his jaw with an exaggerated gesture. "Now, maybe if you give me fair warnin' next time, you and me could have a friendly wrassle, and we'll just see who comes out on top."

"And the loser gets a nice hard spanking from me," Clint chimed in, his eyes dancing.

"Don't you mean the winner?" Jonas quipped.

All Tyler's anger and indignation had evaporated in the face of their easy good humor and he laughed along with them, ignoring for the moment just how far gone his heart was for the cowboy poet.

Clint clapped Tyler on the shoulder. "Okay then," he said. "Now tell us about the vet's assistant. Did you catch him in the act? You got news?"

Tyler, who had completely forgotten about why he'd been seeking Clint in the first place, nodded eagerly. He patted his shirt pocket, but realized with a shock that the camera was gone.

"You lookin' for this?" Jonas bent down and retrieved the camera, which must have fallen out when he'd knocked Tyler to the ground. Jonas wiped the dirt from it against his jeans and handed the camera to Tyler.

"Thanks," Tyler said, anxiously turning it on. To his relief, it appeared intact, all the pictures still saved. Turning back to Clint, he said, "We were right. He was the one. I caught him hauling off a tank in broad daylight. I'll say this for him—the kid's got balls. The sheriff's on his way. Might even be here by now."

Clint pumped his fist in the air. "Boy howdy, that's great news. Let's go see what's goin' on."

Jonas cleared his throat, again rubbing the spot where Tyler had socked him. "Ahem. I think we still got some unfinished business here."

Tyler and Clint turned toward him. "And what might that be, Jonas?" Clint asked with a straight face, though a smile seemed poised on his lips, trying to break through.

"I'm thinkin' we need to teach this city boy some proper country manners. Some kind of punishment is definitely in order."

"You know, Jonas," Clint replied, rubbing his chin thoughtfully, "I do believe you're right. A good old-fashioned over-the-knee spankin' might be just the thing."

Tyler looked from one to the other, not entirely sure if they were kidding or not. He knew one thing for sure, if they were serious, he'd be ready and willing to receive his just desserts.

Chapter 7

Clint was humming along with Patsy Cline on the radio as she sang about sweet dreams of a past love and trying to connect with someone new. Tyler listened to the words, trying not to attach any meaning to them as far as Clint and he went. Jonas had definitely thrown a wrench into their fledgling relationship. Despite Clint's reassurances, Tyler still wasn't entirely sure where Jonas fit into the mix in Clint's mind, or for that matter where Tyler himself fit.

It had been a long day, with the two of them giving their statements down at the sheriff's office, once Steve Buford had been taken into custody. Clint was driving Tyler back to Lubbock, where he could check into a motel.

Clint had invited Tyler to stay with him at his ranch in Ransom Canyon that night, but Tyler had been the one to demur. He told himself it was because he still hadn't submitted his article for the poetry festival, and his editor had sent a rather terse email reminding him of the deadline. He had to buckle down and give it his full attention, something he would never be able to do with the sexy cowboy anywhere in the vicinity.

But if he were honest, there was more to it than that. He'd been thrown for a loop by his own reaction to what he'd perceived as Clint's plight back in the old hay barn. He'd given no thought at all to leaping in to save his new lover, ready, on some level, to give his own life for Clint's.

He couldn't remember in all his thirty years ever falling so fast or so hard for someone. He was head over feet for the cowboy poet, and had no idea what to do about it.

Clint pulled into the parking lot beside Tyler's car and turned to him. "I got to see you again."

"Yeah," Tyler agreed, regretting his decision not to go back with Clint to his ranch then and there. He was on the verge of saying so but Clint spoke first.

"I know you got to finish that article and all," Clint said. "But we got some unfinished business to attend to."

A teasing lilt had entered Clint's tone and Tyler knew at once what he was talking about, though he pretended not to. Every time he thought about the two cowboys in the old hay barn, talking to each other about how he needed a good old-fashioned spanking, the blood rushed to his cock. He could almost feel Clint's hard, calloused hand landing with a wallop on his bare ass.

"Oh, there is?" Tyler suppressed his grin. "What might that be?"

"You know good and well what that might be, boy. Jonas and me'd be derelict in our duties if we let you get away with your bad manners back in the barn. No, sir," he grinned. "We'd be doin' you a real disservice if we failed to give you the punishment you so richly deserve. I'll expect you at my cabin tomorrow night. Eight o'clock suit you?"

Tyler couldn't help it—he grinned back, though a tiny flag of anxiety unfurled in his gut at the thought of Jonas being there to witness the spanking. "Jonas'll be there?" he said with a gulp.

Clint's grin eased into a gentle smile. "If that's okay with you, Ty. Jonas is a good friend. My best friend for nigh on fifteen years now. You matter to me, Tyler. A lot. I want to share with you the things and folks in my life who matter too." Clint reached out and gave Tyler's thigh a squeeze. "Ain't nothin' gonna happen you don't want to happen. Not tomorrow night. Not ever. That's how it is with you and me, Ty. You have my word on that."

"Okay." Tyler still wasn't entirely sure how he felt about Jonas witnessing his spanking, though he couldn't deny the big, burly man was handsome, in a rough and tumble kind of way. But Clint had left the choice open with his words. Nothing would happen that Tyler didn't want to happen.

The thought of being bent, bare-assed, over Clint's powerful thighs, slipped into his mind, sending a shockwave of longing through his body. Not eager to get out of the truck with a hard-on, Tyler forced his brain to switch gears.

He cleared his throat and stared out the window as he got control of himself. "I'm shooting to get the festival article done tonight. Then tomorrow I want to do some background checking on the tank story. I hope to interview the suspect, if the sheriff will let me. And I hope to check out where he lives, take a few pictures, see what I can find out."

Clint nodded. "You might want to talk to the doc too," he suggested. "See what he knows about the kid, in light of all this. He's probably got family locally too. Let me know what's goin' on. I'd be interested in readin' your article."

Tyler smiled, warmed at Clint's interest in his story. They were becoming not only lovers, but friends.

Knowing if he didn't leave the truck now, he'd lose his resolve completely, Tyler reached for the door handle. "Okay," he said, "I'll call you later, let you know what I find out."

"Terrific," Clint replied, tipping his cowboy hat slightly toward Tyler with a nod. "And I'll text you the directions to my place. My cabin's way in back of the ranch—nice and private." He winked. "Remember, eight o'clock tomorrow night. Don't be late, now."

~*~

Clint was bent over the engine of a tractor that had been losing oil around the head gasket. Aside from the fact that it was one of his jobs, Clint enjoyed tinkering with the farm equipment, as it gave him a chance to be alone with his thoughts.

Clint hadn't wanted to let Tyler go the night before. If he'd had his way, he would never let Tyler Sutton go. And yet, that happening was about as likely as them buying a little house with a white picket fence and picking out curtains together. It just wasn't in the cards, not given the life he'd chosen as a rancher in rural Texas. True, he was tolerated in spite of his sexual orientation by the folks who knew him well, but that was about as far as the acceptance went.

It occurred to him, not for the first time, that life as a gay man would be easier in a place like Austin, but even the thought of living somewhere without the vast prairies and wide open skies of his beloved West Texas filled him with a sense of unease. He guessed he was a cowboy first, before anything else, and that was bred into his bones.

And what of Tyler? He'd been raised on a ranch, not much more than two hours from here. He'd had no trouble, so it seemed, in just picking up and taking off for the big city, leaving behind the world and the folks he knew. Yet, Clint sensed Tyler hadn't really left it behind. He'd taken whatever, or whoever, he'd been running from right along with him. He was still carrying demons inside his heart—demons that would continue to haunt him, Clint suspected, until he faced them head on.

Clint found himself almost regretting that they'd solved the tank theft mystery so easily. It had been the perfect excuse to travel together, away from the prying eyes of others as they explored their newfound connection with one another. As Clint adjusted the cylinder valves, he smiled a little to himself, recalling Tyler's immediate assumption and reaction when he'd seen Jonas and himself tussling in the dirt. Clint had once been like Tyler, acting first and thinking later. As the years had gone by Clint had developed a habit of moving slow—taking his time to assess a situation before barreling in with both fists cocked.

Clint was excited by the prospect of the spanking. He knew Tyler was less than certain about Jonas and what role he would play between them. Clint vowed to himself to make it work, not only for him and Tyler, but for Jonas as well.

Clint's cock perked up as he imagined the scene unfolding, with Tyler over his knee, the two of them taking turns at that hard, sexy ass. His cabin offered a good deal of privacy, secluded as it was from the rest of the ranch. Maybe he could convince Tyler to stay a while longer. Maybe they could even leave the ranch, and camp out at his favorite site, a few miles off the beaten trails of the national parks. Jonas and Clint had discovered the spot years ago, a secluded bit of real oasis smack in the middle of the West Texas desert, surrounded by mountains and complete with its own lake.

Clint looked up as he heard the sound of Jonas' truck rumbling down the dirt road that led to Clint's cabin. Clint hopped down from the tractor, wiping his hands on the back of his jeans.

He watched as Jonas climbed out of the truck. He had a cooler in tow, which Clint knew was filled with long-necked bottles of cold beer. Jonas glanced around. "Where's your new friend? We got unfinished business." He grinned.

Clint looked at his watch. "You're early. Eager, huh?"

Jonas laughed, ducking his head in agreement. "You got you a live one there, Clint. I ain't seen you so fired up about anyone since...well, not since we was young."

"We're still young," Clint said with a smile. "And yeah," he admitted. "Fired up is one way of puttin' it. He's under my skin, that's for sure."

They walked together the short distance to Clint's cabin. "I'll be right back," Clint said. "Just goin' to wash up and change. Make yourself at home." He nodded toward the sitting area he'd created out back, which included two sturdy but weather-beaten old chairs across from a low, wide bench. A squat wooden barrel that served as a table sat between them.

Jonas set the cooler on the ground beside the table and reached inside for a bottle. He turned one of the chairs backwards and straddled it, stretching his long legs out on either side. "I'll be waitin'." He tipped his beer and took a long drink.

Clint went inside, glancing around the one-room cabin, with its screened-off bedroom, living area and compact kitchen. His battered guitar was leaning against the scuffed old leather sofa beside a pile of notebooks he used to scribble his ideas and poems in. He glanced at the iron bedstead at the end of the room, imagining Tyler there, stretched out naked.

Turning on the shower, he stripped off his sweat and grease stained clothing and stepped into the stall. He gripped his shaft, imagining Tyler kneeling there at his feet, mouth open, face tilted up eagerly to accept his cock. Forcing the image away, he soaped up quickly, wanting to be outside when Tyler arrived.

Clint dried himself and dressed in fresh jeans and a black T-shirt, trading out his scuffed work boots for his favorite pair of black alligator boots. Glancing at his watch again, he went back outside and sat beside Jonas. He accepted a bottle of beer and took a long swig. He glanced again at his watch, wondering if maybe it wasn't working right, as the hands didn't seem to be moving.

"What time you got?" he asked Jonas, starting to rise from the chair. Maybe he'd just check around front.

"You know I don't wear a watch." Jonas grinned. "Now sit your ass down. He'll get here when he gets here."

Clint sat down. "Maybe I should call him. It's easy to get confused when you're tryin' to get to the back of the property. He's never even been to the ranch. Could be he's lost."

Jonas smiled indulgently at Clint, shaking his head.

"What?"

"You're fidgetin' like a kid waitin' for that three o'clock bell to ring. Relax. He's got your cell number, right?" Clint nodded. "So he'll call if he needs to."

Clint grinned. "You're right. I feel like a kid again, all right. Tyler burst into my life like sunshine into a room I hadn't even realized had gone dark." Clint glanced worriedly at Jonas, afraid he'd take offense to that remark, where none was meant. "Hey, I didn't mean—"

Jonas cut him off with a smile. "I know you didn't, buddy. It's me, remember? We got our own special understandin'. We're friends first, don't forget that. I know I won't. I'm happy for you. Truly I am." His face clouded a little. "That is, it's great to see you so excited about somethin'. He's got to be pretty special, to have affected you like this. I can't remember when you've been so riled about someone new. But, I guess I'm wonderin'..." he trailed off.

"Wonderin'...?" Clint prompted.

"Well, he's a city boy, right? In the area on assignment, but then what? You gonna start some long-distance thing? How's that gonna play out? Have you thought of that?"

"Sure, I've thought of it," Clint said, annoyed, though he knew that wasn't fair. Jonas was only pointing out what he'd been thinking about himself. He forced a laugh. "Shit, listen to us. I've only known the guy a few days and you got us movin' in together. You that eager to get rid of me?"

Jonas shook his head. "You know better than that, Clint." Clint did know better. He could no more imagine his life without Jonas in it than he could imagine living in New York City.

Clint jumped up. "You know, I think I better wait in the front of the cabin. He might not realize we're out back."

Jonas chuckled and nodded. "You go on. You ain't gonna rest till he gets here."

Clint walked to the front of his place and waited, sipping his beer and letting his mind drift. Jonas was right—he was riled all right. He couldn't seem to get enough of the eager, sexy young man who had fallen into his life like a gift from the heavens. They'd only been apart a day and already it felt like way too long.

It was only a few minutes after eight when Tyler's car appeared at the bend in the dirt road. Clint waved and Tyler, catching sight of him, waved back. He parked his car and climbed out. He looked good, real good, in a tight white T-shirt that molded against his broad shoulders and barely contained his biceps.

As they approached one another, he could smell the scent of fresh soap on Tyler's skin. He resisted his impulse to take Tyler into his arms then and there, still mindful of being on the ranch, even if they were far from prying eyes. Once in the back of the cabin however, he wrapped his arms around Tyler as he bent him back in a kiss that left no doubt who was in charge.

He could feel the change come over Tyler as he kissed him—the easing of Tyler's muscles as he surrendered into Clint's grasp, his lips parting, his cock hardening against Clint's thigh. He loved the way Tyler responded to the control he exerted, and it just made him want him all the more.

When he finally let Tyler go, Clint was momentarily surprised by the sound of Jonas' voice. He'd actually forgotten Jonas was there. "Whoo wee," Jonas laughed. "The two a' you got it bad."

Tyler whirled toward Jonas, flushing slightly. "Oh," he said, shoving his hands into his pockets. "Hi Jonas. I guess I didn't see you there."

"No, I reckon you didn't. Y'all only had eyes for each other." Jonas grinned, winking at Clint. Clint had a moment's worry—was Jonas as okay with this as he seemed? He studied his old friend's face a moment, but saw nothing there but Jonas' big smile.

Jonas stood and moved toward Tyler, holding out a bottle. "Care for a beer?"

"Thanks." Tyler took it as thw three of them settled in chairs, Jonas again straddling the back of his.

"So, how did the investigatin' go?" Clint asked Tyler. "Did you get to talk to that rascal?"

Tyler shook his head. "Doc Crawford posted his bail early this morning. I went by the trailer park where he lives, but I couldn't get anyone to answer the door. I took a few pictures but that was that. I did talk to the doc, who filled me in some about Steve's life. He's barely twenty and has no family to speak of. His father was a heavy drinker who died young and his mother just passed away last year from cancer. He's got a sister off in Houston or somewhere but she never makes it back home. Doc Crawford has kind of taken Steve under his wing, so he took this thing pretty hard. He said Steve's short on judgment but underneath it has a good heart.

"Apparently Steve wasn't even aware of the value of the semen he stole. He was more focused on the worth of the tanks themselves, and was turning them over to this older guy who lived in the same trailer park and had talked Steve into doing the thefts for some quick cash. That guy's been picked up for questioning, and they got a warrant to search his trailer. Looks like he was trying to make meth, or some fool thing. Some of the tanks were still there and will be returned to their owners."

"Well, that's good news," Clint said. "At least the thefts will stop now." He smiled at Tyler. "I guess we made a pretty good team, huh?" "To the cowboy crime fighters," Jonas said, lifting his beer bottle in salute. He handed them each a fresh bottle and they watched the sun setting bronze against the darkening sky as they drank their beer. Bullfrogs and cicadas serenaded them in the purpling twilight.

Tyler leaned back in his chair. "This is the life," he said with a contented sigh. "I didn't realize how much I missed the country since I moved to Austin."

"What made you leave?" Jonas asked.

Clint watched the struggle work its way over Tyler's face as he formed an answer. Tyler hunched his shoulders a little and took a long drink before answering. When he finally spoke, it seemed to Clint he wasn't saying what was uppermost in his mind.

"Well, my standard answer is I always wanted to be a writer. A reporter on a newspaper with a beat of my own. I actually got a degree in journalism—well," he amended, "I minored in it, while studying animal science at A&M."

"You didn't tell me you'd hooked up with a brainiac," Jonas said to Clint with a wink.

"Nah." Tyler scowled. "I went to school because my father said so. I would have rather stayed on the ranch, riding the horses all day. But he was bound and determined someone in the family was going to college, and that someone happened to be me. I'm not sorry, in retrospect, but at the time I just saw it as one more way for him to control me."

"Sounds like maybe you left the ranch to assert your independence too," Jonas observed.

"Yeah." Tyler glanced at Clint and then stared at the ground. "You could say that, I guess."

"You miss ridin'?" Clint asked.

"Something fierce. I haven't seen Star, my mare, since I left six months ago."

"You haven't been back since then?" Jonas asked.

Tyler shook his head. "My sister, Sarah, takes good care of her. We talk on the phone from time to time. She'll never leave the place. They'll take over one day, if my dad ever hands over the reins."

"Well, we got a couple good horses in the stables, Ty," Clint said. "How 'bout I'll hook you up in the morning for a nice ride? Nothing like watching the sun rise while on the back of a horse with the wind flyin' at your back. We get out early enough, I'll have time to go with you."

"That'd be great." Tyler turned a grateful smile in Clint's direction, who smiled back.

After a while Jonas turned to Clint. "Look-a-here," he said, flashing a grin as he rubbed at his jaw. "I do believe I got a bruise from that boy of yours. We were gonna do somethin' about that, weren't we? A paddlin' to teach the boy some manners?"

Clint laughed, taking up the thread. "Why, we sure was, Jonas. Good thing you reminded me. I bet Tyler here is more than ready to make up for his misdeeds. Right, Ty? You ready for that spankin' we promised you?"

Chapter 8

Tyler looked from Clint to Jonas and back to Clint, his heart suddenly in his throat. He'd been so focused on researching his story and writing up his notes that he'd almost forgotten the sexy promise of the spanking.

He stood, backing away from the two cowboys, a nervous grin breaking out on his face. "Gosh," he said, stalling for time. "I was so busy today. My mind's been on other things."

"That's okay," Clint said, his dark eyes gleaming. He stood as well. "We remembered for you. Might as well take it like a man."

"Yes, indeed," Jonas said, rubbing his big hands together with such exaggerated glee that it made Tyler laugh, despite the bubbles of nervousness that had suddenly popped into his stomach. "You can throw a punch like a man—let's see how well you take what's comin' to ya'."

"You'll have to catch me first, old man." With a laugh, Tyler turned, making a sudden sprint toward the copse of trees that edged the property.

"He must be talkin' 'bout you, Jonas," Clint laughed.

"Oh, yeah?" Jonas roared in mock anger. "We'll just see about that." Moving faster than his girth should have allowed, in seconds Jonas was on Tyler, catching him from behind in a bear hug that actually lifted Tyler off the ground.

"You're gonna pay for that old man comment," Jonas bellowed. Tyler tried to twist out of the strong man's arms, but dissolved into embarrassed laughter when Jonas blew raspberries on the back of his neck.

When Jonas set him down Tyler twisted suddenly, ready to sprint away again, but this time Clint was right there in front of him, blocking his retreat. All three of them were laughing as they tussled, but Tyler was no match for the two of them.

Between them, they wrestled the still struggling and laughing Tyler back to the wide bench. Clint sat down on one end of the bench and maneuvered Tyler across his knees. The bench was low enough and wide enough that Tyler's head was hanging off the end of the bench and nearly touched the grass on one side of Clint, his ass on Clint's lap, his legs stretched out along the bench.

Jonas knelt down on one knee in a kind of crouch in front of Tyler's head, catching his wrists in one big paw. Tyler pulled against Jonas' iron grip, a sudden clutch of panic rising in his gut. While he couldn't deny that something about being held down as he was sent a jolt of pure lust hurtling through his cock, at the same time he knew deep down it was wrong. What was it that made him long for this type of rough treatment? What sickness lingered inside him that made it, for him, so much more than a game?

Tyler lifted his head, locking eyes for a moment with the big man, wondering if Jonas, or Clint for that matter, had any idea of the depths of his need to feel the pain and submit to the humiliation. If they knew, would they still be laughing?

"Lucky boy," Jonas mouthed, winking broadly at Tyler, and Tyler knew for certain that for him it was just a game.

Clint leaned over him, his breath warm on Tyler's cheek. He must have sensed something in Tyler's demeanor or body language, because his voice was gentle, its tone coaxing. "Hey, relax," he said. "We're just havin' fun, okay? If it doesn't suit you, say the word." As Clint spoke, he pushed his hand up under Tyler's T-shirt, stroking his back. The hand moved down, massaging his ass cheeks through his jeans.

Clint's touch was like fire, lighting all Tyler's nerve endings. Oh, it suited him all right. That was the problem. His heart was beating fast and he caught his breath. Lust and need overrode any philosophical concern of his own moral fiber or lack thereof. He wanted what these two sexy cowboys were offering, and he wanted it bad.

"Yeah," he managed, his voice throaty. He jerked hard against Clint's legs as Clint's palm landed hard against his ass. Despite the denim that covered him, he could feel the powerful sting. Jonas held his wrists fast.

Clint struck him with a series of blows that made Tyler's cock harden into pure steel as it rubbed against Clint's legs. For a moment he had the terrible feeling he was going to come in his pants. He wriggled some, trying to take the direct pressure off his cock but it only made things worse.

He was distracted by Clint's words to Jonas. "You're the one he took a swipe at. Care to even the score?"

"Thought you'd never ask." Still holding Tyler's wrists in one hand, Jonas brought the other down hard on his ass, the palm cupped to add an extra wallop. This was followed by a series of lighter smacks that seemed to be coming from both men at once, covering both cheeks in rapid-fire succession.

Just when Tyler didn't think he could take another lick, Jonas sat back, and Clint began to rub Tyler's burning ass cheeks with a soothing, easy touch that calmed him some, though it did nothing to ease his raging erection.

When Clint finally let him up, Jonas let go of his wrists and Tyler rolled from Clint's lap to the dirt. Clint was watching him with that fiery gleam in his eyes that made Tyler want to get to his knees and wrap his arms around Clint's legs right then and there.

Clint stood and moved behind Tyler. "Stand up," he ordered, his raspy voice rolling like sex over Tyler's senses. "We ain't done with you, boy."

Tyler scrambled to his feet, confused and excited, not sure what to expect next. Clint grabbed his arms, locking them behind his back and Jonas, as if on cue, knelt in front of Tyler.

Looking up at Clint, Jonas reached for Tyler's crotch, covering the very evident bulge with one large hand. "I declare, Clinton," he said with an evil grin. "I sure would like to get a taste of that. Yes, indeed." He rubbed his palm over Tyler's bulge.

Clint pulled his arms back harder, forcing Tyler's back to arch, his groin thrust forward. "That suit you, boy? You took your correction like a man. Would you like a reward? Jonas here is very skilled in that particular department. He'll make you forget all about that stingin' ass of yours."

Jonas reached for Tyler's belt buckle. "Clint," Tyler pleaded, trying to twist away. "We're outside. Someone could see."

Tyler's heart was going a mile a minute. Wayne had done this, or something like it, forcing Tyler to suck him off out behind the barns where anyone could have stumbled upon them. Though he couldn't deny the thrill of possible exposure, he'd resented Wayne's refusal to listen to his concerns.

But this was different. He didn't know anyone on this ranch, and besides, his cock was so hard it probably wouldn't take more than a few strokes before he came. Beyond that, he was thrilled at what was happening to him—it touched the core of some of his deepest, darkest fantasies.

"Nah," Clint said, unaware of his inner turmoil. "Nobody ever comes back here behind my cabin. Anyway, we'd hear 'em if they tried. Don't you worry, Ty. You're safe. I would never do somethin' to put you at risk."

He drew his tongue down the side of Tyler's neck, drawing an involuntary shudder from him. "You earned this, boy. Just relax and enjoy it."

Jonas looked up at Tyler, smiling broadly. Tyler gulped and then nodded his consent. He wanted this too damn bad to protest any further. His cock was bent uncomfortably in his jeans, aching for release. He sighed with relief when Jonas unbuckled his belt and pulled opened the metal buttons on his fly. Hooking his large thumbs beneath the fabric at Tyler's hips, Jonas yanked both the jeans and Tyler's underwear, dragging them to his knees.

"This here is mighty fine." He stared at Tyler's cock and balls with open appreciation that only made Tyler's cock harder, if such a thing were possible. "Mighty fine," Jonas reiterated.

Clint held Tyler's arms fast behind him. He could feel Clint's erection pressing against the small of his back as Clint leaned forward, lightly biting Tyler's neck.

Jonas looked up at Clint, a question in his face. Clint spoke behind Tyler. "Use your hands first. Stroke him, light and easy. Take your time. I'll let you know when you can taste the goods."

"Yes, Sir," Jonas said, eyes bright. His use of the word "sir", and the fact he was the one on his knees, reminded Tyler of the dynamic of their relationship. Though Clint said they were now just friends, the lines remained sharply drawn, with Clint clearly the one in control.

He stopped thinking altogether when Jonas' big hand closed over his cock, pulling up and drawing the skin taut before moving down again in a perfect friction. Tyler moaned and then gasped as Clint lightly bit and then licked his neck. "You're mine, boy," Clint murmured.

"Now?" Jonas growled, his mouth hovering near Tyler's fisted cock.

"Now," Clint agreed.

Jonas' lips slid wetly over the head. Tyler let his head fall back against Clint. Jonas moved lower, taking the full length of Tyler's engorged cock into his mouth. "Oooo," Tyler moaned, his legs going weak with pleasure as Jonas licked, kissed and sucked his cock. He cradled Tyler's balls in one hand, letting one finger trail along toward the sensitive pucker between his cheeks.

As Clint kissed his neck, Tyler twisted back, searching hungrily for Clint's mouth with his. Their lips met, tongues entwining while Jonas continued to suck and stroke Tyler's cock. Tyler gasped against Clint's mouth as Clint pulled back hard on his arms, reminding him he was restrained. Jonas gripped Tyler's shaft in his hand as he nuzzled against Tyler's crotch.

Tyler was dizzy and hot. Sweat was trickling down his sides. "That's it, baby," Clint murmured, as Tyler began to shake. He heard someone moaning and realized it was himself. His balls tightened against Jonas' relentless, sweet attack and his climax rose, fast and hard.

"Fuck," he breathed. "I'm gonna come."

"Not yet." Clint emphasized his words by tightening his grip on Tyler's restrained arms. "Hold out for me. Wait till I say." A part of Tyler thrilled to Clint's command, making it that much harder to control the impending climax.

He forced himself to ease off, willing his body to delay its pleasure a little longer, despite Jonas' continued and focused attention at his crotch.

When Clint reached beneath Tyler's sweat-soaked shirt, finding and twisting his nipple, the zing of sensation ricocheted directly to his cock. Tyler let out a cry that was part pain, part nearly unbearable pleasure.

"Now, boy. Come for me. Do it." Clint's voice was a low, sensual growl in Tyler's ear.

And suddenly Tyler understood. This was *it*—that strange, elusive thing he had always longed for and never quite achieved at Wayne's cruel hands. On a deep, primal level that defied words or understanding, the sweet pain, the low seductive voice of his dominant lover and the rising tide of orgasm combined together to wrest from him his complete surrender. He let go, jerking against Jonas' grip, giving in to the climax that overtook him, rising up from his groin and ripping through his body like a tornado.

Clint let go of his nipple and wrapped his strong arms around Tyler from behind, holding him close. Tyler sagged against him, leaning his head back into Clint's chest. His legs felt like rubber and his heart was pulsing in his ears.

When he could focus, Tyler saw that Jonas was smiling up at them. Tyler smiled back weakly. "Wow," he managed to croak. "That was something amazing."

"It sure was," Jonas agreed with a grin. "For a second there I thought you was gonna take off like a rocket and lift all three of us clean up into the sky. Whooo weee, you got you a live one there, Clint."

"We got us a live one, all right," Clint agreed. "But something tells me you had more than a little to do with that, Jonas." Tyler, still held up in Clint's arms as he tried to recover from the most powerful orgasm he could ever remember, nodded his agreement. He held out his hand and Jonas took it, surprising him by planting a quick kiss on his palm.

"Jonas," Clint added, still supporting Tyler with one arm as he reached down to ruffle Jonas' hair, "you've been my best friend for a long time. I'm honored you can still be my boy from time to time." A tiny barb of jealousy poked into Tyler's gut, but he barely felt it, held so close in Clint's arms.

"And Ty." Clint nuzzled his chin against the side of Tyler's neck. "I didn't even realize I was lackin', but havin' you in my arms is like comin' home."

Still holding tightly to Jonas' big hand, Tyler twisted his head back and kissed the bottom of Clint's chin, a surge of affection rushing through him. He was safe in Clint's arms, possessed in the best of ways. Something was moving through him, opening and easing that part of him inside that was always coiled tight. It took him a moment to identify the feeling.

He was happy.

~*~

Clint let Tyler go and stepped back. Tyler swayed a little but was otherwise reasonably steady on his feet. Jonas stood and bent down, pulling up Tyler's jeans and underwear with a laugh. "The skeeters are comin' out in force, Ty. You don't want 'em bitin' areas best left covered."

"No sir," Clint agreed, laughing. "I think we need to move this party inside, don't y'all agree?" Neither Jonas nor Tyler offered any protest, though Tyler still seemed lost in a blissful, post-orgasmic fog.

Once in the cabin, the thought of stringing both his boys up, side by side and naked, had a definite appeal, but before he could act on this idea, Jonas said, "Now it's your turn, Clint. Me and Tyler here will show you a right good time, won't we, Ty? You just set back and relax and leave it to us."

Clint glanced at Tyler to see his reaction. If he seemed hesitant or uncomfortable, Clint would step in and make it right for him, whatever that took. But Tyler only nodded, a slow, sexy smile edging its way along his lips. Maybe the combination of the beer and the orgasm had relaxed him enough to move forward, or maybe he was just getting more comfortable with the situation.

"Yeah," Tyler said eagerly. "I'm the only one got any, uh, satisfaction. I want to return the favor."

"Well, that's good, very good, Ty," Clint said with a smile. "And don't you worry. We both intend to get our satisfaction, you can rest assured. We got all night. Jonas and I aren't quite so wet behind the ears," he teased. "We know how to wait for what we want."

"Hey, that's not fair—" Tyler began, but Clint only laughed and pulled him into his arms.

"I'm just teasin' you, Ty. You were perfect out there. And if you're willin', we'll just keep right on goin'. Would that suit you?" He brushed Tyler's ear with his lips.

"Yeah," Tyler said, relaxing against him. "It would suit me fine."

The three of them shucked their boots and tossed off their clothing, leaving it in small heaps around the room. Clint couldn't help but smile as he watched Tyler's eyes move down toward Jonas' cock, which was in proportion to the rest of his body, huge even in its present state of semi-erection.

Jonas was also apparently following Tyler's gaze. A grin broke over his face as he reached for his cock. "Like what you see, boy?" Clint was at once amused and touched by the sweet flush that suffused Tyler's features as he looked away.

It was clear Jonas planned to run the show, which was fine by Clint for the time being. Jonas sometimes like to exert control, but they both knew that for him it was just a game, and a way to show his affection. In the order of things, Jonas would always be his boy.

But Tyler was becoming more than just his boy—he was becoming his lover, and where did that leave them come morning?

Shaking away this thought, Clint allowed Jonas to direct him to the bed, where he lay on his back across the old hand-stitched quilt. "On your belly," Jonas directed. "We got to work out the kinks before we service you properly. Your job right now is to lie still and hush. Think you can handle that?" Jonas asked teasingly.

"I think I can manage it, *boy*," Clint drawled, adding emphasis to the last word to remind Jonas of his place, though he too was teasing. He rolled over, stretching his arms over his head with a contented sigh. Jonas had a way of easing those strong fingers into the muscle, rubbing out the kinks, as he called them, until a body fairly melted.

"You sit on this side," he heard Jonas say to Tyler, "and I'll be over here." The two men settled on either side of Clint on the bed. He remained still, his eyes closed. "I'll take his back, you take his ass and legs. Take your time and use your muscle. Clint likes it hard, don't ya', boy?"

Clint growled his laugh. "Watch your step, Jonas. You'll find yourself trussed and hogtied before you know it."

"Promises, promises," Jonas replied. "Now hush and take what's comin' to ya'."

Clint sighed his appreciation as strong fingers dug into the muscle at his shoulders. Tyler's hands moved lightly over his ass and down his thighs. Tyler's touch made his cock harden beneath him and he lifted his hips slightly to adjust himself.

Tyler strengthened his touch some, kneading the flesh of Clint's ass and thighs as Jonas continued the deep tissue massage on his shoulders and back. Clint gave himself over to the sensations as two sets of powerful hands rubbed and eased every stitch of tension from his body. He was drifting and sliding down into a half-dream state but was too contented to do anything about it.

Then he felt himself being flipped over, limp as a ragdoll. He opened his eyes and groaned as Jonas leaned over his chest, flicking at his nipples with a warm tongue, while Tyler closed silky lips over his erect shaft.

He luxuriated in the sensations for a while, but as Tyler licked and sucked, the familiar, welcome rush of dominance reasserted itself in Clint's consciousness and he sat up, gently but firmly pushing both men away.

"That was heaven, boys, and I thank you. But unless you want to knock me out for the night, we gotta change things up a bit." He gripped his erect cock and ran his tongue over his lips. "I still expect your full attention, but for now I'm runnin' the show."

Jonas grinned, used to Clint's taking over. Tyler was watching him with shining eyes and parted lips. Both men's cocks were as hard as his own. Clint felt the power of his position like a rush of pure adrenaline kicking up in his blood.

He focused on Tyler, looking deep into those very blue eyes. "I want you Ty, I want you bad. I want to feel your mouth around my cock. I want you to take me so deep I can feel your throat swallowing my cock. Do you want that too, Ty?" He stroked Tyler's cheek, still gazing deep into his eyes. "Do you want to please me? Will you let me take you the way I want to? Will you let me take your breath away? Will you trust me to take you there and back again safely?"

His eyes fixed on Clint, Tyler took a deep breath, swallowed hard and nodded his consent.

Clint slid off the bed and stood, energized with excitement. "Ty, you lie flat on the bed, head hanging just off the edge here." He pointed to indicate what he meant. "Jonas, you straddle Ty's hips and keep that cock of his hard, you hear?"

"From the look of things, that shouldn't be a problem," Jonas quipped, staring pointedly at Tyler's full erection.

The two men moved quickly to obey, Tyler stretching himself horizontally across the mattress, his head hanging just off the side as Clint had indicated. Jonas climbed over Tyler's hips, his erect cock brushing Ty's as he positioned himself.

"Your job, Ty," Clint growled softly into Ty's ear as he knelt down beside him, "is to worship my cock and balls with your mouth. I want you to stay focused on me. Open yourself to me, trust me. I'm gonna give you my cock slowly at first, and I want you to stay relaxed. When I get goin', I'll go deeper. Would you like that, boy? To feel all of me? I may go so deep that it'll block your breathin' a bit, but I won't give you more than you can handle. If you feel like it's too much, just raise your hand and I'll stop. I may be runnin' the show, but ultimately you call the shots. Okay?"

"Yeah," Tyler said in a throaty whisper.

Clint kissed Tyler, thrusting his tongue deep as a prelude for what was to come. Tyler responded eagerly, moaning against his mouth. When Clint let him go, he noticed the drop of pre-come at the tip of Tyler's cock. Jonas had noticed it too. He licked his lips and grinned at Clint, raising his eyebrows in unspoken question.

Clint nodded toward Jonas. "That's your job. Keep him hard while I use his mouth, but don't let him come."

"Yes, *Sir*," Jonas said, the delighted anticipation fairly glowing on his face. He leaned down, closing his lips over the head of Tyler's cock.

"Focus, boy," Clint reminded Tyler. "Your job is to pleasure me and take what's given to you. Don't initiate anything. And you will *not* come, understand? Not unless or until I say so, no matter what Jonas is doin' to you."

Tyler nodded, gulping, and Clint smiled, well aware of that curious reaction guys like Tyler experienced when told they couldn't come—they immediately and desperately wanted to do just that. He understood too, that the sexual suffering this engendered was pure pleasure—pleasure he was glad to give.

He met Jonas' eye a moment and Jonas gave a small nod of acceptance and approval. He'd meant what he'd said earlier about being happy for Clint, and his last bit of anxiety over hurting Jonas' feelings slipped away. Clint stood again, leaning over Tyler to lightly kiss Jonas' lips.

The bed was just high enough for what he had planned. By bending his knees slightly, his cock was at the perfect angle to ease down into Tyler's open mouth. As he inserted the head, Tyler at once began to suckle and lick.

Jonas caught Tyler's shaft in one hand, the other loosely wrapped around his own formidable cock. Tyler moaned against Clint's cock. "Focus," Clint reminded him. He teased Tyler's lips, allowing only the head of his cock to move past them. To his credit, Tyler did focus, licking and kissing whatever Clint offered him with eager abandon.

Slowly Clint pushed downward, allowing Tyler to get used to the length of his shaft before pressing farther. This time he was the one who groaned with pleasure as Tyler expertly milked his cock.

"You like havin' my cock in your mouth? You ready to take more for me, boy?" He stroked Tyler's bare chest, grazing his nipples with his fingertips. He rested one hand for a moment on Tyler's rapidly beating heart.

"You ready?" Clint asked again, pulling back so Tyler could answer.

"Yeah," Tyler murmured, his eyes fluttering shut, his hands still resting loosely by his sides. Jonas was focused on Tyler's cock, as instructed, his mouth and hands busy.

Clint leaned forwarding, guiding his shaft back into Tyler's mouth, this time pushing farther downward than before, not stopping until he pressed past Tyler's soft palate. Tyler stiffened and Clint could feel his momentary panic. Clint pulled back enough to allow Tyler to suck in some air and settle himself.

"Relax," he soothed, pressing his hand gently against Tyler's smooth chest. "Don't fight it. This is about the trust, Ty. Let go."

Tyler stilled, his body easing. Jonas continued to stroke Tyler's cock with one hand, his own caught in a loose grip in his other hand, his brown eyes fixed on Clint's glistening shaft.

Clint lowered himself once more into Tyler's open mouth, again not stopping until the head of his cock lodged against the back of Tyler's throat. Clint savored the feeling of his cock engulfed in the velvet warmth of Tyler's mouth and throat. Tyler handled it better this time, opening his throat to accept Clint's cock, allowing his windpipe to be blocked in a supreme show of trust that thrilled Clint to his bones.

He pulled back slowly, his hands moving over Tyler's chest. Tyler again began to lick and suck at Clint's shaft. Clint pulled all the way out, looking down at his lover, whose eyes were closed, his mouth open, hungry as a baby bird.

This time Clint shifted slightly, moving closer to offer not his cock, but his balls, for Tyler's attention. Tyler licked in fevered circles around the delicate skin as Clint teased him, hovering just high enough to make Tyler work to reach him.

He nodded toward Jonas, who picked up the tempo and friction at Tyler's groin, pulling a groan from Tyler's mouth that vibrated against Clint's balls. He lowered himself, allowing Tyler to take the entire ball sac into his mouth.

Tyler eagerly accepted his offering, licking and sucking at Clint's balls until his cock felt like it would explode. Pulling back, Clint again eased his shaft into Tyler's still-open mouth.

"You have no idea how hot you are right now, Ty," Clint said. "You make me feel so good. And you're such a brave, courageous boy, lettin' me claim you like this with my cock. Stay loose and easy. You're doin' fine, just fine."

Gauging Tyler was ready for more, Clint slid into the hot, welcome clutch of Tyler's mouth. He pushed farther, cutting off Tyler's air, holding his own breath at the same time to make sure he kept Tyler safe.

When he finally drew back, Tyler gasped, sucking in a bushel of air, but he kept his mouth wide open, his arms resting loosely at his sides.

"Wow," Tyler said softly, staring up at Clint with something that seemed to approach love. "I feel like I just went somewhere. Somewhere like heaven. I'm still floating from it. It's fantastic." The awe in his voice touched Clint's core.

At last, he thought with amazement. *I found my kindred spirit at last.*

Jonas was watching him. Clint wondered if Jonas knew what had just transpired between Tyler and himself. It was a connection he'd once dreamed of having with Jonas, but they'd never managed to go there. Still, the friendship ran deep, and Jonas was sexy as all get-out.

Jonas still gripped both Tyler's cock and his own, pumping them in tandem as Clint

fucked Tyler's eager, hot mouth. When it was too good to hold back another second, he gasped, "Do it. Come for me, both of you."

Jonas was breathing hard, a flush rising up his neck, a sheen of sweat moving over his powerfully muscled chest as his hands flew over Tyler's cock and his own. Tyler moaned against Clint's shaft, his tongue doing things that had to be a crime, it felt so damn good. Within second,

Jonas arched forward with a cry, streams of hot, white semen shooting over Clint's hand and Tyler's stomach and chest.

Somehow he managed to keep working Tyler, who began to buck as he spurted. Clint groaned, stiffening as he ejaculated deep into Tyler's throat. He pulled back, his cock sliding from Tyler's mouth, and fell forward, landing beside Tyler on the bed.

Breathing hard, he shifted until he was head to head with his lover, curled against his back, his arm thrown over Tyler's shoulders. Jonas stretched out behind Clint with a long, satisfied sigh.

Tucked between the two men, Clint drifted a while in post-orgasmic bliss. He was sandwiched between Jonas and Tyler, and the symbolism of their positions made him smile. Jonas was behind him and Tyler before him. Jonas was a part of his life, as comfortable as an old horse blanket, while Tyler was new and elusive, the thrill of mutual discovery still before them.

Yet Tyler was only passing through. The problem was, on the way he'd somehow managed to snag Clint's heart. Lying there between the two men, Clint couldn't help but wonder—what happened now?

Chapter 9

"This here's Toby." Clint patted the sorrel's soft nose as he slipped the halter over it. "Seven-year-old gelding with an easy disposition." Clint led Toby out of his stall and walked down toward the blue roan in the next stall over. "This is Lady. She's got a lot of energy and a fiery nature, but under the right hand she gentles up nice. Which one you want?"

He turned to Tyler, smiling inwardly when Tyler chose Lady, as Clint had guessed he would. They led the horses out of the stalls and into the paddock, looping their lead ropes over fence posts. The sun wasn't quite up yet, but its approach was turning the night sky to gray, tinged with lavender.

Clint brought their saddles from the tack room and Tyler took Lady's, expertly saddling her up while he murmured softly to her. Clint watched him a moment, admiring Tyler's easy way with the sometimes temperamental horse. He approached her with the natural confidence of a lifetime rider, but beyond that Clint sensed his immediate affinity with the animal.

"She takes to you right nice," he observed, as they mounted the horses and turned in the direction of the trails at the back of the ranch.

"Feels good," Tyler said. "It's been too long since I was on a horse. Way too long."

They rode alongside the pasture's edge toward the wooded trails.

They went in single file, Clint leading the way. He should have been tired, as they'd had very little actual sleep the night before, but he felt energized and more alive than he'd been in years.

After the impromptu threesome with Jonas, they'd sat out back again for a while, sharing another beer. Before leaving, Jonas had wrapped them both in a big bear hug. To each of them he'd said the same words, a large smile on his open face. "You take care of him, you hear? He's definitely a keeper." Then he'd left them for the night.

Once he'd gone, Clint had asked Tyler, "You gonna stick around for that sunrise?"

"You bet." Tyler's smile warmed him, and they soon returned to the cabin, where they stripped and fell naked together into the bed. Their lovemaking was by turns hot and fierce, and then slow and tender as they drifted between sleep and a hunger for each other that was like nothing Clint had ever experienced.

If he had his way, Tyler would never leave, but he well knew real life was coming soon to intrude, and he did his best not to leap there before he had to. Instead he held Tyler in his arms, watching him sleep, his strong, handsome face outlined by the silvery light of the moon, until he finally gave in to the tug of slumber.

They came out of the copse of trees and moved toward an outcropping of stone beside some wild grass that was good for grazing. Dismounting, they tied the horses to a nearby tree and moved to sit on the stone ledge, facing east. They couldn't have timed it better. The top curve of the sun suddenly appeared, a shimmering crescent of pure gold. They watched in awed silence as it pushed its way over the edge of the horizon, filling the sky with a sudden, blazing light.

"That's somethin' I never tire of seein'," Clint remarked.

"It's been way too long since I've seen a prairie sunrise." Tyler's voice was wistful, even sad.

Clint looked at him, studying his face from the side. "Why'd you really leave, Ty? What're you runnin' from?"

He felt Tyler stiffen and almost regretted the question, but if there was something developing between them, he needed to know what it was that held Tyler back. Clint remembered how powerfully Tyler had protested the first time he'd exerted his dominant will—*I don't do this. I told you, I ain't nobody's boy.*

Though Tyler's reactions to their play had been powerful and sincere, Clint continued to feel an underlying resistance from him. It was almost like Tyler was longing to surrender, but believed that doing so would prove him the weaker man. There was something, or someone, holding him back.

Tyler was a man fighting with himself, not comfortable with his own nature. This fight was going to continue to affect their relationship, unless they found a way to deal with it head on. What they'd shared was too special to ignore or deny. He could no longer pretend to himself that Tyler was just passing through, or that Clint had no business poking his nose where it didn't belong. Somehow he needed to find a way to reach Tyler, before it was too late, before he returned to Austin, never looking back.

This was his chance, and he had to grab it. They could either choose to move forward together, or let it end. Clint prayed he could somehow prevent that from happening. He didn't want to just let Tyler slip away. There had been other men, other potential, and he'd let them slip away, telling himself the time wasn't right, or the man wasn't worthy.

He understood in a moment of clarity that he'd let them go because he wasn't willing to fight for love. Now, for whatever reason, he found that he was. He was ready to claim what he wanted for his own. If he wanted this thing with Tyler, whatever it was, he had to at least try.

And so, when Tyler did his usual, stiffening and turning his face away with a shrug, Clint leaned toward Tyler, grabbing him gently but firmly by the shoulder. "Ty. Don't shut me out. Talk to me. We have somethin' special, you and me. And it's not just about who's on top and who holds the whip. We got somethin' that doesn't come along too often. Are we just gonna let it go?"

Tyler turned slowly toward him, though he still didn't speak. "Ty," Clint tried again. "You're safe with me. Haven't I showed you that over this past week? But you've got a wall up between us. It's something only you can tear down. What really happened back at the ranch that has you runnin' not just from the ranch, but from yourself?"

Tyler turned back toward the horizon, staring out into the middle distance as if he didn't even see the riot of glorious color splashed over the sky. Clint could see a muscle working in his jaw, as if the words were stuck, trying to find a way out. Finally Tyler said cryptically, "I'm not the man you think I am."

Clint waited, refusing to permit himself to leap to any conclusions. When Tyler didn't continue, he prodded gently. "Go on."

Tyler glanced at him and then quickly away. "There was someone. He was like you. But he wasn't like you. I mean, you make it seem okay, but I know deep down it's not okay. This isn't how a man's supposed to act. Supposed to feel…"

"Ty, what are you sayin'?"

Tyler turned toward him. "Look, it's been a great week. You're a terrific guy. But this whole thing—the ropes, the commands, the spanking and stuff. I know for you it's just this hot, sexy game. But it's not right for me. I've been down that road before. I know what ends up happening. I can't live my life like that. I'm a man, damn it. Not someone's whipping boy."

Clint felt as if he'd been slapped, but he forced himself to remain calm. Tyler was confused—scared. That was all this was. "This ain't a game, Ty," he said slowly. "Not for me. It's who I am. I see who you are too, and we fit together." Tyler started to speak, but Clint cut him off, determined to have his say.

"Ty, you were born for this. You can deny it all you want, but you were born to submit and I was born to give you what you crave. We're like, I don't know, we're like two pieces of a puzzle, if you will, that fit together. We fit each other's groove. We're kindred spirits, you and me. You need the pain to be intertwined with the pleasure, and I need the rush I get from claiming and earning your trust. You give up control and I take it. It's part of a powerful circle of give and take. You gotta trust what's happenin' here, Tyler. You gotta trust yourself. What you're feelin' isn't a sign of weakness. It doesn't make you a lesser man. In fact, true submission is about courage, about giving yourself over in a way that is powerful and strong. Let me take you there, Ty. Let's explore our deepest urges and needs together. I've been waitin' all my life to find you. Don't shut me down. Don't shut *us* down just because you're afraid of what you don't yet fully understand."

Tyler was staring at him as if he were speaking in tongues. Frustrated, Clint tried again. "Look, Ty, just because you had a bad experience—"

"You aren't listening to me," Tyler shouted. "It's more than a bad experience. It's me. I make bad choices. I choose men who treat me like shit. You use the guise of sexual games but in the end it's about control. You just said it. I give up control. Well, I'm not willing to do that. Not this time. I learned my lesson, and it was a hard one."

Tyler blew out an angry breath and continued. "Wayne started out playful too, but when it got rough, when I wasn't comfortable, he kept pushing, same as you're doing now. And I let him. Don't you see? I let him do it. I was so into the rough play, and so lonely and desperate for that connection, that I let him treat me like shit, and tried to tell myself it was just part of the fucking game."

Tyler stood abruptly, moving away from Clint. He scrambled down the rocks and walked rapidly toward the horses. Both horses looked up. Lady whinnied softly and pawed the ground with one foot, clearly agitated by Tyler's tone and rising voice.

Tyler turned back to face Clint, a flush of anger rising up his neck. "There's something wrong with me. Something twisted up that you can't fix." Tyler unhitched Lady and put his foot in a stirrup, swinging himself up onto the saddle. "Don't you see—I let him take me over, same as you want to do. Then I turned and ran, tail between my legs. I'm not the man you think I am, Clint. I'm not a man at all. I let him run right over me, like I was some kind of weak, pathetic loser. You might think I'm this kindred soul, or whatever you called it, but how long before you realize just who you're really dealing with? Better you find out now, and cut your losses. Better you go back to Jonas, where it's all comfortable and easy and you can play your games and find other guys to bring into your little threesomes."

Clint reared back, stunned and hurt at Tyler's words, and the venom behind them. What the hell had just happened? How had things skidded so fast into something so wrong? "Ty, please. You got to hear me."

"No, you hear me." Tyler crossed his arms over his chest. "I'm done being played for a fool. I know the real deal. Your type just wants to take. You just want to take me over. Well, not this time. Not this time, Clint Darrow. You and that friend of yours, y'all picked the wrong guy."

Tyler jerked the reins, turning Lady back the way they'd come. Clint watched in stunned disbelief as the best thing to ever happen to him disappeared among the trees.

~*~

"I especially like the article about the bull semen theft, Tyler. I sent back some edits and suggestions. You did a good job on both articles. You've got the makings of a real investigative reporter."

Tyler smiled, trying to bask in the warmth of his editor's praise, but the pain of his confrontation with Clint still moved in his gut like jagged pieces of glass, cutting him to the quick. What the hell had happened back there?

"Thanks, Angela," he managed. "I'll be back in Austin later today. I'll look at the revisions as soon as I get in."

His editor hung up. Tyler stared unseeing at the traffic on the freeway, his mind returning to earlier that morning.

The whole thing had been surreal. It was almost like he'd been watching himself from a distance, staring in frozen horror as he took out his own stupid insecurities and the whole mess with Wayne and dumped them like a big, steaming pile of horse shit right into Clint's lap.

"You did it again, Sutton," he said aloud as he drove. "You're an asshole and you deserve what you get. Wayne knew it. It was just a matter of time before Clint figured it out, too. You just sped up the process, is all. Just as well. He can say what he wants, but he's probably still in love with Jonas anyway. There isn't room for me there. I was just passing through."

He gripped the steering wheel tight with both hands, blinking away the angry tears. What was wrong with him? Clint was nothing like Wayne. Tyler knew that, yet he'd tried to paint them both with the same broad brush. The look of hurt and pain on Clint's face had nearly ripped the heart right out of Tyler, yet he'd been unable to stop his diatribe, too ashamed of himself and what had happened with Wayne to risk letting Clint know the real truth. If he ever found out what Tyler was really like deep inside, he'd run as fast as he could in the other direction. Better for Tyler to run first.

He thought about Wayne's sneering retorts when he'd half-heartedly tried to change the dynamic of their twisted relationship before the whole thing blew up.

"You're just a piece of ass, Tyler," Wayne had told him. "A piece of ass who knows his place, which is at my feet and on your knees. Got it?"

How Tyler had chafed at this—rejecting it in his heart and mind, while at the same time craving the biting lick of the lash and the feel of Wayne's sharp palm on his ass. It was this conflict—this uneasy balance between humiliation and raw desire that had kept him tethered to a man who was bad for him.

He'd made the break, true, but he'd done it by running. He'd abandoned his family and his work on the ranch, not because he really wanted to be a reporter, but because he was too scared to face his own demons.

Tyler closed his eyes a second, losing the battle to block the painful memories as the humiliation of that last, horrible confrontation between them forced its way into his consciousness, as vivid and real as if it had just happened.

It had been their usual meeting place and time—late at night when the rest of the ranch was sleeping. They'd met in the tack room off the stables, the place where Wayne had first exerted his brand of sadistic control.

Wayne had used the riding crop, thoroughly whipping Tyler's bare back and ass on that cold February night until he was on fire. He knew from experience he'd be bruised the next day and was glad for the cover his flannel shirt and jacket would afford him.

Wayne had laughed at Tyler's erection, telling him he was a sick puppy who deserved everything he got. He'd pulled his cock from his jeans and ordered Tyler to suck him off, but instead of coming in Tyler's mouth, he'd shot his load over the dirt floor and then pointed. "Lick it up, faggot. Go on, do as you're told."

Faggot.

That word, spat with such derision, set something off in Tyler, a small, bright blaze of anger that for once actually overpowered his twisted submissive compulsion. Leaping to his feet, he'd shouted, "I'm gay, Wayne. So are you. Why do you want use a hateful word like that?"

Wayne sneered at him. "*I* ain't gay, you faggot. Gay, fag, what's the difference what you call it? It's what you are. On top of the beatin's you deserve, you take it up the ass and suck my dick. What do you think that makes you?"

The anger tightened in Tyler's chest, coiling like a rattlesnake ready to strike. "And you, you're what?" His hands had clenched into fists at his sides. For the first time, he actually considered taking Wayne on in a fight. He was bigger than Wayne, but he suspected Wayne was the kind of guy who would fight dirty. He had the kind of wiry, coiled energy that was fueled by anger and egged on by a need for power. He was, Tyler suspected, someone who would fight to win, no matter the cost.

"I ain't no faggot," Wayne snapped. "No man's ever been near *my* ass. But *you*," he sneered the word. "Not only are you queer, but you get hard from bein' beat. You jerk off alone to the memory of suckin' my dick and takin' my whip. You're one sick motherfucker, and you know it and I know it. You better watch your step, *boy*, or everyone else will know it too."

It was this threat, more than anything else, that had made Tyler's blood run cold. He'd never come out to his family, not about his sexual orientation and certainly not about this sick compulsion to submit at the hands of a man like Wayne Hurley. He understood in that instant that Wayne held all the cards. Wayne might get fired, but Tyler would lose everything if Wayne went public with their relationship.

He'd taken the coward's way out, packing his bags and heading as far away as he could think of. He'd used all his savings those first few months, augmenting the crappy minimum wage of the lousy jobs he managed to procure to afford the cost of living in the big city, before lucking into the *Lone Star Monthly* gig.

He'd lied to his family, claiming it was something he'd been needing to do—to find himself on his own terms as a writer and independent person. His mother had pleaded for him to come home. His father had been angry, talking about the money he'd wasted educating Tyler to run the ranch better, and ranting about the irresponsibility of Tyler's generation.

Tyler hadn't spoken to his father in months, though his sister and mother kept him updated on the goings-on at the ranch. A discreet inquiry on his part confirmed Wayne Hurley was still gainfully employed at the ranch, and now it was too late for Tyler to do a thing about that. He'd made his bed by running away, and now he had to lie in it.

Then there was Clint.

Clint Darrow, the sexiest, kindest, most exciting man Tyler had ever met. He made submission seem like a good thing, something consensual between lovers. Maybe it was, between well-adjusted, normal guys like Clint and Jonas. They were longtime lovers, confident in themselves and each other's affections. Tyler doubted they harbored the dark, secret need he had to experience pain as a part of his pleasure. If Clint really knew how intensely Tyler longed for the whip and the rope, would he still want to stick around?

And what about Jonas? Yeah, the sex had been hot, and the spanking even hotter, but what was the real deal there? Maybe Tyler was just one in a long line of boys the two of them picked up, separately or singly, as a part of their own kinky play. Yeah, Clinton had done a good act of convincing Tyler he was special, but the fact of the matter remained—Jonas had been on the scene well before Tyler, and no doubt would be long after Tyler was nothing but a bad memory.

It was better that he left when he did, though he still regretted his hot-headed reaction to Clint's questioning. If only he'd kept his cool, deflecting the questions and just parting with a kiss and a promise to keep in touch. That would have been so much easier. He could have let Clint fade away in his mind. He could have returned to the gay bars and the guys named Jeff or Jim who disappeared from his consciousness the moment after they said goodbye.

Well, despite the fact Clint still loomed large and constant in his mind and heart, he'd get over him. It was for the best. It was time to take back his manhood and push all this twisted submissive shit back to its hiding place deep in his psyche.

Tyler Sutton was nobody's boy.

Chapter 10

"Did you just hear a word I said to you?" Jonas stood towering over Clint, the exasperation ripe in his tone.

"What? Yeah, I heard you," Clint mumbled without looking up. He continued to whittle the stripped branch in his hand, scraping curls of soft wood with the side of his pocket knife, honing it to a sharp point. When he was done, he would poke it upright into the damp earth beside the other sticks he'd worked on.

"What did I say, then?" Jonas demanded.

It had been five days since Tyler Sutton had put an end to the best week of Clint's life, leaving as abruptly as he'd appeared that night at the festival, disappearing without a trace from Clint's life, though certainly not from his heart.

Clint looked up slowly from his whittling. "You said I'm a damn fool for lettin' him get away. You said you wished you had been there 'cause you wouldn't have just let him ride off like some damn cowboy in an old Western."

"That was ten minutes ago. What I said was, you need to get up off your ass, quit feelin' sorry for yourself, gas up that old pickup and drive to Austin to fetch his ass and bring him on back."

Clint said nothing. He'd thought of that a hundred times over the past days, and each time he'd talked himself out of it. He had his pride.

He'd done nothing wrong. Tyler was the one who had made assumptions and then run with them, not even having the grace or courtesy to let Clint respond to his unfair accusations.

Tyler's words still cut across his mind like a blade, drawing blood from his memory each time he relived that horrible scene.

I'm done being played for a fool. I know the real deal. Your type just wants to take. You just want to take me over. Well, not this time. You and that friend of yours, y'all picked the wrong guy.

His type.

Somehow Tyler had cast him as some sort of demon—someone who used guys like Tyler, exploiting their submissive needs instead of honoring and nurturing them. That Tyler could have so misread him and then to unfairly accuse him of crimes Clint could only imagine rankled like a burr under his saddle.

When Clint could get past his own pain he understood this guy Wayne had done quite a number on Tyler—somehow convincing him he was dirty and less-than because of his submissive bent, instead of someone special and to be cherished. He tried to tell himself it wasn't Tyler's fault—he was reacting off that prior pain, incorrectly tarring Clint with the same brush he used in describing that bastard, Wayne.

"Damn it, Clint. There's gonna be no living with you until you do something." Jonas again interrupted Clint's reverie. He wished Jonas would just go away and leave him to his misery. Life was hard enough without Jonas to rub in how he'd fucked up by letting Tyler go.

Sure, it was easy for Jonas to say just go get him. But Clint knew better. He'd seen the rage in Tyler's eyes and felt the fury of his accusations. The knife slipped, its sharp tip pricking the tip of Clint's index finger. He watched the droplet of blood form with a detached disinterest.

"Goddamn it, Clint. I ain't never seen you like this. It's like all the life's been sucked clean out of you." Jonas plopped down beside Clint on the old log. Clint wiped his finger on the back of his jeans and went back to his whittling.

Jonas had tracked him down to his favorite hiding place—the place he went when he needed to be alone and think, which was all the time since Tyler had gone. It was a stream sheltered by a few trees, out behind his cabin on the edge of the property. The sound of the rushing water was soothing, and he liked to pick up old branches and break them down, whittling the pieces for no particular purpose but to distract his mind.

Jonas put his hand on Clint's shoulder and squeezed it gently. Though Clint was truly grateful for Jonas' friendship, right now he fervently wished he would just go away. He meant well, but he didn't understand.

Clint was thirty-nine years old and facing the first real heartbreak of his life. How the hell was he supposed to deal with that?

As if reading his thoughts, Jonas offered, "Come on, Clint. You've faced hard times before. I've watched you do it. When your mama was wastin' away from the cancer, you were there every step of the way, seein' to her care, fightin' for her needs when they tried to cut off the insurance. When Joe nearly lost the ranch due to that lawsuit with that idiot buyer, you were the one who stood up to him and made the case disappear. Ain't what you found with Tyler worth the work? You gonna let some confused boy with his head up his ass get the better of you? You gonna let yourself be beat down because he's too stupid to look love in the face and know what's he seein'?"

"Love," Clint repeated, rolling the word on his tongue, testing its strangeness. It wasn't a word he used lightly. He'd never told Tyler he loved him, not in their brief but intense week together. Had he ever told anyone that?

"That's right. Love. You're as hardheaded as Tyler in your own way, Clinton Darrow. You're in love with that boy, and I'd bet my bottom dollar he's in love with you, but he's too dumb to see it. It's up to you now. You gotta show him. You get in that truck and you drive to Austin. You knock on his door and you tell him. Tell him what's in your heart. If you don't, you'll regret it for the rest of your life."

Clint finally looked at Jonas, really looked at him now, at his open, kind face with its earnest, pleading expression. For the first time since Tyler had ridden away, the bitter ache of his hurt was soothed a little. "You think?" he finally said.

Jonas nodded emphatically. "If you don't go find him and at least try to talk some sense into him, then you're givin' up without a fight. You *never* give up without a fight. Not the Clint I know." Jonas smashed his closed fist on his thigh for emphasis, and then continued.

"There's somethin' you said to me once, Clint, when I was bein' a fool over some guy I was too scared to go after. I don't even remember the guy now, but I sure do remember what you said."

"Yeah?" Clint smiled in spite of himself. "And what was that?"

"You said, '*If only*. Those must be the two saddest words in the world.'" He paused, letting the words sink in. Then he added, "You were right, Clint. Don't let that be you. Not this time."

~*~

That Friday morning Tyler lay half in an erotic dream, vaguely aware of the steady beeping of the alarm, but not yet ready to return to full consciousness. He reached a hand toward the clock, blindly seeking the snooze button so he could dive back into the sensual net of the dream.

He missed, catching instead the glass of water he vaguely remembered pouring for himself at about three that morning, when he'd woken up dehydrated from his dinner of scotch on the rocks. The glass went flying to the floor, splashing him as it fell. The glass didn't break, at least, but the water and the crash succeeded where the alarm had failed, jerking him fully awake.

"Fuck," he snarled as he swung his feet over the side of the bed and sat up, glaring at the overturned glass as if it were at fault. He rubbed his hands over his face. His eyes felt gritty and his mouth tasted sour. As he had every night the past week, he'd drunk himself into a coma that resembled sleep, trying to blot out the misery of his life.

He'd returned to Austin feeling more wretched than he thought possible. Nobody in the history of the human race could be a bigger jerk than he was, he'd decided. He'd behaved like a horse's ass with Clint, blaming Clint for his own shame and confusion.

But what he'd done couldn't be undone or unsaid. It was too late. He'd blown it. Clint Darrow was, without a doubt, the best thing to ever happen to him, and what had he done? Ruined everything with his own insecurity and hardheadedness.

He'd thought of calling or texting Clint a hundred times. He'd even gotten so far as pressing the numbers into his cell phone, but he'd stopped himself each time. There was no way Clint would want to hear from him, not after how he'd behaved.

Clint had probably relayed the whole sorry mess to Jonas after Tyler had wheeled on his horse and galloped off. At the time he'd been so upset with himself he couldn't even think straight. He'd returned Lady to her stall, hung her saddle in the tack room and jumped into his car, aware he was running, though he wasn't even entirely sure what he was running from.

As he made the long drive back to Austin, he'd had plenty of time to think about just what it was he was running from, and had come to the sad realization that no matter how far he went, he was still stuck with himself.

There was something wrong with him, and he told himself it was better that he'd left Clint when he had, before Clint figured out his desires went deeper than just erotic play.

That's all it was for Clint and Jonas, he'd decided. A sexy game they played. They'd included Tyler because after all, beggars can't be choosers. It wasn't exactly like the pool of gay cowboys into rough play was exactly huge in rural West Texas. Tyler had flattered himself that he was something special. In the end, though, the pickings were slim and so he got picked.

Yeah, Clint talked a good line about it taking a strong man to submit, but did he really understand when it overtook a body like a sickness? Did he know Tyler dreamed of being bound and beaten—that it made his cock hard just to say the words?

While these thoughts raged like a summer twister in his brain, his heart cried out that he was a fool. Clint had treated him with nothing but kindness and care, reassuring him every step of the way that his feelings were natural and okay, even admirable. But that was only because he didn't know the real Tyler Sutton—the one who ran instead of facing his fears. The one who ran instead of facing feelings that, if acknowledged, might cause more heartache than he was prepared to risk.

On some level he knew he had run so that Clint couldn't run first. He'd only forced the inevitable, and he'd done it in the nick of time, before he did something really stupid like admit he was falling in love.

His cell phone was vibrating on the nightstand and for one ridiculous moment hope flared like a beacon in his chest—Clint.

But it wasn't Clint. No, who was he kidding? If Clint had been going to call, he'd have done so by now. He had probably washed his hands of the whole sorry affair, and laughed with Jonas about what a loser that Tyler Sutton had turned out to be, and good riddance.

He touched the screen. "Hi, Angela." His voice came out thick with sleep. He cleared his throat and tried again. "What's up?"

"Jesus, Tyler, you still asleep? It's after ten o'clock. We missed you at the staff meeting. Again. You've hardly been at the office all week. Where's the article on that new folk art museum over on South Congress you were supposed to have on my desk by yesterday?"

"Oh, shit," Tyler began. He'd forgotten all about that assignment. Before he could come up with a credible excuse, Angela barreled on. "What the heck's going on, Tyler? I thought you were back in town. Are you still on assignment in Lubbock, for heaven's sake? Am I confused? I had this strange idea you worked for this magazine on salary, not as some freelancer who sent in stories when it suited his fancy. Carl was expecting you to fact-check his story on charter schools. Carl doesn't ask for just anyone. When you weren't there, he went to Melinda instead. Last month you couldn't *wait* to work with our lead writer. What the hell's going on?"

"I'm really sorry, Angela. I've—I've been under the weather. I'm not thinking straight. I'll be in later this morning. I was just headed out the door."

"Yeah, well you better *start* thinking straight. This is the big time. You finally got your first byline in *Lone Star Monthly*, the national magazine of Texas. But you're only as good as your next story, kiddo. You've got real potential as a journalist, but this is a professional operation and we run on a timeline. Don't blow it. There's plenty of interns just waiting for their opportunity to pick up the ball if you drop it."

~*~

When Tyler finally left the magazine's offices at around eight that evening, he was beat. Operating in a hangover-induced fog, he'd cranked out the article on the museum, doing a half-assed job, before turning to the boring, tedious job of fact-checking Carl Hick's lead article on how charter schools were fundamentally changing the Texas education system. His heart just wasn't in his work, and Clint Darrow kept invading his thoughts, despite his best efforts to shut him out.

Five cups of coffee over the course of the day, along with a greasy hamburger and fries hadn't improved matters, and it was a relief to finally stumble out of the concrete and glass building in downtown Austin to the large black-topped employee parking lot. The lot was mostly empty now, though a few of the more dedicated staff were still on the job.

The magazine was a good place to work, and Austin was a great city, as far as cities went, but it wasn't the country, that was for sure, and he found, especially after the last week back in West Texas, that he missed the wide, open spaces and the green plains of home more than he'd realized.

During that all-too-brief ride on Lady, his body had leaped awake to the feel of the saddle and the horse's easy, powerful grace beneath him. He missed his own horses. He missed the air free of car exhaust and city smells.

He missed Clint.

He missed him so bad that he actually thought for a split second that he saw Clint's beat-up old pickup truck parked beside his car in the lot. As he got closer, he saw it was even the same model and color as Clint's truck.

He saw someone was slumped in the driver's seat, their face obscured by a cowboy hat, tipped down against the setting sun. His heart did a sudden summersault in his chest when he saw the silver band against the black felt of the hat. Either his longing to see Clint had actually conjured the man's hat, or Clint Darrow was sitting in the parking lot of *Lone Star Monthly*, asleep in his truck.

Tyler walked to the driver's side of the truck, his heart going a mile a minute. His mouth was dry and prickles of perspiration popped beneath his arms. What was Clint doing three-hundred-seventy-five miles from home? More to the point, what was he doing parked beside Tyler's car?

Tyler's mind was short-circuiting as he tried to comprehend what he was seeing. Even as the elusive and uncontrollable emotion called hope began to balloon inside him, he moved to quash it. He tried to tell himself he didn't *want* to see Clint again. Clint knew his dirty secrets. He had understood and exploited Tyler's desperate need to submit, but he didn't understand the depth of Tyler's shame.

Maybe this was it then—the chance to really lay it out there. Once he understood the full extent of Tyler's humiliation at the hands of Wayne, and how little he'd done about it, Clint would thank his stars Tyler had turned tail and run.

The windows were open and Tyler leaned lightly against the doorframe, staring at the man in repose. He looked at him a long time, at the work-roughened hands that rested on either side of him, at the powerful thighs and the sexy bulge at his groin, covered in faded blue denim that was soft as calf skin from a thousand washings. He looked at the curling V of chest hair visible at the opening of the denim work shirt and at the slightly pointed chin and sensual lips of the sleeping man.

He drank in the sight of the guy who had occupied just about every waking moment of his life since he'd met him. Clint Darrow was never out of his thoughts, either playing front and center when Tyler was alone and brooding on his own stupidity, or pushed down to a steady, aching hum just beneath the surface when he managed to force himself to concentrate on tasks that no longer interested him.

As if aware of the intensity of Tyler's hungry gaze, Clint shifted against the seat, pushing his hat back up on his head as he slowly opened his dark, sleepy eyes.

He turned toward Tyler, a smile moving its way over his mouth.

"Hey there, Ty," he rasped.

"Hey," Tyler responded, no other words coming to his aid as his stomach twisted. He wanted to look away but found he could not. He was drawn to this man like a moth to a flame. Heat fanned through his body, a heat that had nothing to do with the temperature outside, and his muscles tightened in anticipation, though of what, he wasn't entirely sure.

Jesus God, I want this man. I want him something awful.

The words echoed so loudly through his head that for one terrible second Tyler thought he'd said them aloud.

They stared at one another for a long while and Tyler realized with a jolt that Clint's look was just as hungry as his own, as if he were memorizing the features of Tyler's face, as if he might never see him again.

Finally Tyler found his voice. "You're a long way from home," he observed. Clint nodded, not helping him at all. "What, uh, what brings you to Austin?" Tyler added inanely, feeling like a fool.

"You."

"Oh."

After a long paused, Clint added, "You gonna stand there all night or you gonna get in?"

Tyler found that his body was better at taking direction at that moment than his mind, which still couldn't quite seem to get a handle on what was happening. His legs were carrying him around the back of the truck to the other side. His hand was pulling open the door and then he was climbing in, settling beside Clint, his own car forgotten.

Clint was watching him. Tyler wished he would say something, anything, but Clint remained silent.

"I was a horse's ass," Tyler finally blurted.

"Yeah," Clint agreed somberly.

But as Tyler watched, a smile broadened on Clint's face and there was a gleam in those dark, sexy eyes. Tyler found himself smiling back, and realized he hadn't smiled in a week—his cheeks actually ached with the unfamiliar effort.

And then he was grinning, and so was Clint. Laughter bubbled up in a rising joy from somewhere deep inside him, pushing its way past his lips. Clint began to laugh too. They laughed for a long time, the kind of freeing, raucous laughter that brings tears and sighs as it subsides, only to be kicked off again by a glance.

Finally they sat in silence, but it was an easy silence, the tension broken by their laughter. Tyler ventured, "You came all this way to see me?"

Clint nodded. "Sure did. I never did like to let a man get in the last word. We got us some serious talkin' to do, Ty."

Tyler's heart sank. Clint had driven all this way to lecture him about what a jerk he had been. Clint was still laboring under the delusion that Tyler was a better man than he was. Clint just didn't understand, and Tyler was going to have to lay it all out. The irony was, once he'd told Clint the cold, hard truth about himself, Clint would no doubt cut his losses and head home. Yet Tyler was no longer willing to lie, or gloss over his own shameful past and continued sordid longings. If nothing else, he owed Clint the unvarnished truth.

He turned toward Clint, all the joy of the moment before evaporated in the face of his trepidation.

But Clint was smiling again. He reached for Tyler's face, pulling him close and kissing his mouth. With Clint's touch, the dread and sorrow that had been weighing in Tyler's heart lifted, and he let himself fall headlong into that kiss, wishing he could freeze this one perfect moment in time forever.

Chapter 11

Clint followed Tyler to his apartment house, a sterile looking three-story cement box wedged in between other cement boxes on a busy street not far from the magazine's offices. The apartment itself was nice enough, if rather bland, with a beige sofa and matching chairs, and beige wall-to-wall carpeting. There were no pictures on the walls and no personal knickknacks in the built-in shelves along one wall, as if Tyler hadn't really moved in all the way yet.

Clint noticed the empty bottle of scotch whiskey on the glass coffee table and several more empty bottles of booze on the bar that served as a separator between the living room and the kitchen. He said nothing about it, however, as Tyler pointed toward one of the bar stools and said, "Can I get you something? I have a few beers in the fridge. I don't really cook much but I think I have some chips and salsa left if you're hungry."

"A beer would be fine," Clint replied.

Tyler, standing on the other side of the counter, leaned forward suddenly, grabbing the empty bottles from in front of Clint with a swipe of his arm. "Sorry. I wasn't, uh, expecting company."

"You mean you drank those all on your own?" Clint couldn't help but ask.

"Uh, yeah, I guess." Tyler sounded embarrassed, and then added in a more belligerent tone, "Is there a law against drinking in your own home now?"

Clint didn't rise to the bait, instead merely noting in a mild voice, "Looks like maybe you had as rough a week as I did. That's all I meant."

Tyler slid a beer bottle across the counter toward Clint and twisted the lid off a second bottle. "Oh. Yeah, I guess you could say that." He took a drink of his beer and set it down. He remained standing, the counter between them like a protective wall.

Clint wished they were sitting on the sofa instead, or better yet, lying together in the bed in the room beyond, but he could see Tyler was anxious and edgy, the sweetness of that shared kiss in his truck no longer in play.

Had he made a mistake, driving all this way? Had he believed Jonas' staunch assurances that Tyler loved him, not because it was based in fact, but because he simply longed for it to be so?

Well, he was here now, and even if he made a complete fool of himself, he had to try. There would be no *if only*, not this time.

He had thought long and hard while driving to Austin about what his plan of attack should be. A number of possible scenarios had passed through his head, from simply showing up at Tyler's door and hauling him off to the bedroom, caveman style, to demanding an explanation for his outrageous behavior that morning and refusing to budge until he got a satisfactory answer. But bullying Ty and insisting on answers he wasn't ready to give would only backfire in the end. Tyler had to come to him on his own. He had to feel safe enough to find his own way back.

Clint moved toward the sofa. He settled back with his beer, doubting Tyler would mind if he rested his boots on the coffee table. He noticed the narrow glass sliding door and the small railed-in patio beyond it, lit by the glaring lights of the parking lot, and wondered if Tyler could see the stars at night.

Leaning over the bar, Tyler called out, "Want another?"

"I barely started this one," Clint said, shaking his head. He found he didn't really have a taste for it, and set the mostly-full bottle on the table.

"Well, I'm having another," Tyler announced, turning back toward the refrigerator.

"Come over here," Clint said gently, patting the cushion beside him.

Tyler came around the counter and moved toward him, holding the beer bottle against his chest like a shield. He sat on the edge of the sofa, perched as if he might jump up and run at any second.

Clint stroked Tyler's back, which was rigid with tension. He leaned forward, reaching with both hands to lightly massage Tyler's shoulders. He was glad when Tyler set his beer on the table and leaned back a little, letting his shoulders relax some beneath Clint's touch. They were both quiet as Clint continued the massage, and then he offered, "I almost didn't come here. I almost let my own pigheadedness get in the way of seein' you again."

"So…" Tyler let the word hang before adding, "why did you?"

Clint continued to knead Tyler's muscles, moving his hand down Tyler's back and pressing his fingers along either side of Tyler's spine. Tyler let out a deep breath and seemed to relax just a little more. "It was Jonas who talked some sense into my head," he replied. "Sometimes that's what it takes—a friend who can see things we can't. Someone to push us along when we aren't quite ready ourselves to do the right thing."

"Jonas?" Tyler sounded surprised. "But I thought you two…"

"Are more than friends?" Clint supplied, shaking his head.

"Yeah." Tyler nodded glumly. "I mean, you've been together so long and all. The way you brought him into our play and us so new…"

"I'm sorry, Ty, if that was a mistake. I love Jonas, but not in a romantic way. We really are just friends. I think maybe we're too much alike to ever be more than that. But I should have been payin' more attention to where you were at. I guess I thought what you and I shared was strong enough to handle bringin' him into the mix. I see now I rushed you. I didn't take the time to respect what was right for you. I'm sorry 'bout that. I truly am."

"I appreciate that, Clint. I thought I could handle it too. I never used to consider myself the jealous type." He shrugged, offering a small smile, then added, "Okay. So why did Jonas think you ought to come to Austin? To try to talk some sense into my head about all this?"

"No."

"Then what?"

"Because…" Clint took a deep breath. It was now or never. He wasn't fool enough to repeat Jonas' assertion that Tyler loved him, but he could speak his own mind and say what was in his heart. For the first time in his nearly forty years, he would open himself up in the most vulnerable way possible. He would prove to Tyler he meant what he said about everything.

"I'm in love with you."

Tyler twisted toward him, his mouth dropping open in surprise.

Clint rushed on. "That don't mean I got expectations. I don't. I heard what you said that morning when you left. In fact, I've heard little else in my head this past week. I've tried hard to figure it out, Ty. To understand where you're comin' from."

Tyler looked down. Clint continued, "You said some hard stuff and it's etched into my memory, even if I wanted to pretend you never said it. You told me you felt like a loser, and that's the last thing you are. You told me to cut my losses and go back and play my little games with Jonas. If I didn't get nothin' else from that, I understood I failed to show you what I feel for you is way more than just games, Ty. It means everything to me.

"You said you were done being played for a fool, and that my type just wants to take, and to take you over somehow, to make you my object. Your words cut me to the bone, Tyler. I'm not gonna lie. I let bitterness and hurt get in the way of tryin' to understand just what it was that led you to this place. I turned inward instead of reachin' out to you. I let you go when I should have followed." Clint reached for Tyler's hand, relieved when Tyler let him take it.

He squeezed it, and laid his heart on the line yet again. After all, what did he have left to lose? "I'm also here as your friend, Ty. I want to understand. I'm here with open arms and open heart. I'm gonna stay as long as you let me. Not because I expect you to love me back, but because I want to prove that my words haven't been empty."

He stood, pulling Tyler upright along with him as he reached for him. They moved into each other's arms. They held each other wordlessly for a long time, each nestling his head against the other's shoulder, arms wrapped tight around each other. It was as if, by holding tight, they were anchoring themselves to the world, to this moment. It felt so good, so right, to have Tyler in his arms again. He never wanted to let go.

If only he could reach Tyler, really get through to him that what they had wasn't dirty or shameful, but something to be cherished and experienced with joy. He had to keep trying. Jonas was right—they were worth it.

With his head still resting on Tyler's shoulder, he said softly, "If you get nothin' else out of our time together, please hear me on this. Our special kind of lovin' ain't about abuse or humiliation. It's about strength and the courage to give oneself in a loving exchange of power. I'm gonna try my best to prove that to you, if I can. If you'll let me."

By mutual accord, they pulled back, but only so they could lean forward again, this time face to face, lips touching. Their kiss was long and sweet, an exploration, a getting reacquainted. They fell back together on the sofa and Tyler turned to Clint, a small, uncertain smile on his face. "I missed you something awful," he said.

"Yeah? You and me both. I was half-scared you'd tell me to go to hell, but I had to take my chances. You mean too much to me to just let you go without a fight."

"I don't know what to say." Tyler's voice was barely above a whisper.

"It's okay. You don't have to say nothin'." Clint stood and faced Tyler, his hands held palm up. "For what it's worth, I ain't never said those words to another man before. All I got to give you is myself. I don't know what else to tell you. If you want me to go, I'll turn around now and walk out that door. You won't see me again. But if you want me to stay, I got something I want to give you, something I didn't know until we met that I was savin'."

"And what's that?" Tyler whispered.

"My heart."

~*~

I'm in love with you.

Tyler rose from the couch, reaching for Clint's hand as his words echoed through Tyler's mind. They walked together across the room, Tyler leading the way to the bedroom. Neither spoke as they kicked off their boots and shucked their clothing, their eyes never leaving each other.

They stood naked before one another, and Tyler's heart twisted in his chest. "Clint." He wanted to say more, to speak as eloquently as Clint just had about trust and love, but no other words came. And so he said it again. "Clint."

Clint simply nodded, as if he understood what Tyler barely understood himself, as if he could hear the words still locked in Tyler's heart. They moved together toward the bed, pulling back the sheets as they lay side by side.

Clint started to reach for him, but Tyler pushed him back against the mattress. He felt infused by a strange, quiet fire, a certainty, a knowing that he hadn't had before. He rolled toward Clint, his body pressed against Clint's side as he ran his finger over Clint's lips and moved it along his chin. He traced his way along Clint's Adam's apple and down to his collarbone. He pressed his palm gently against Clint's chest, feeling the strong, steady pulse of his heart.

Clint was watching him with a dark, fierce gaze and Tyler could feel that the same quiet fire was burning in him as well. He ran his hand down Clint's stomach, moving along his thigh to the long, jagged scar, which he traced with two fingers, feeling the ridged flesh that marked the old injury and hid the damage done inside.

Tyler moved his hand, tracing inward along Clint's thigh toward his groin. He closed his hand around Clint's cock, feeling it harden and lengthen in his grip. His cock responded in kind, but he wasn't focused on himself. Leaning down, he closed his mouth over the head, licking the drop of milky sweetness that appeared there. He sucked the length of the shaft into his mouth, lowering his head to take it all, then lifting again to let it almost, but not quite, fall from his lips.

Clint moaned as Tyler continued, moving slowly down and back up again along the smooth flesh. After a time, Clint arched up with a shudder and then pushed Tyler gently but firmly away.

He pressed Tyler back against the bed, so he was lying on his back as Clint had been a moment earlier. Clint rolled on top of him, his heaviness like a sensual blanket that both excited Tyler and made him feel safe, all at once. Clint kissed his mouth, his tongue moving as if searching for something as he caught a handful of Tyler's hair in one hand, gripping hard. Tyler groaned against Clint's mouth, the pull at his scalp a trigger that sent him fast and hard into a place that he both feared and desired.

Clint slid off him, reaching with his other hand for Tyler's cock. His stroke was easy at first, his fingers moving lightly over Tyler's hardness. Tyler groaned again, lifting his hips, aching for more. Clint obliged, gripping the shaft with a surer hand, pulling upward and stroking downward, as he used his other hand to pull Tyler's head back by the hair.

He broke off the kiss, though his hands remained at their tasks, making it hard for Tyler to focus on Clint's words. "I want you, Ty. I wanted you from the moment I saw you. Somehow I'm gonna reach you. I promise."

Releasing Tyler's hair, Clint bent down, taking Tyler's cock into his mouth. Tyler groaned and shuddered, willing his body to slow down. Clint was relentless, sucking, licking and stroking his cock and balls.

"Oh, man," he finally cried. "I'm gonna—."

Clint pulled abruptly back. "Fuck me," he said, the words a command.

Tyler's impending orgasm receded as he tried to process what he thought he'd just heard. Clint was a top, a dominant, someone who did the fucking, not the other way around. Tyler was confused. He must have heard it wrong.

As if privy to his thoughts, Clint said, "I told you, Ty, it ain't about who's on top and who's on bottom. It ain't about one person exertin' his will over the other. Not everything's about control, okay? We're just two lovers who want to share ourselves with each other."

Tyler nodded as Clint rolled onto his back, his erect shaft jutting upward. "I want to feel you inside me, Ty. I want to give myself to you in that way. It makes me no less of a man." Tyler slowly nodded again, a glimmer of understanding penetrating the shame he'd held around himself like a cloak for so long. He reached into the nightstand drawer for a condom and the lube.

He slipped the condom over his shaft and squeezed some KY on his fingers. Lying down beside Clint, he gently massaged the lubricant into the tight passage, which eased against his fingers.

"That feels good," Clint murmured. He rolled to his knees and moved over Tyler, pressing him flat against the bed as he straddled his hips. He positioned himself over Tyler's cock, shifting until the head nestled at the cleft of his ass. Placing his hands on Tyler's shoulders, he eased himself slowly down.`

Tyler's cock slipped inside the hot, slick grip of Clint's ass. Clint continued to press down slowly, causing Tyler's cock to slide deeper. He kept his dark eyes fixed on Tyler's face as he began to move in a slow, sensual rhythm over him. It felt fantastic, the clutch of tight muscle massaging his engorged cock.

He looked into Clint's face, catching his breath at the intensity and power of Clint's unwavering gaze. There was such raw tenderness there, such naked vulnerability. Tyler had always thought of men like Clint, men in control, kept a tight rein on any such emotion. He himself had struggled to keep a similar rein, thinking that to do otherwise was to be less of a man.

Yet Clint was every inch a man, his courage and determination evident in everything he did. Even seeking Tyler out after Tyler had walked out—that hadn't, Tyler understood now, been an act of desperation, but one of love and compassion. He had reached out where a lesser man would have just turned his back.

"Clint, I..." Tyler faltered, the words he longed to say hovering just beyond his grasp. Instead he managed, "It feels so good...so good."

As Clint rode Tyler, Tyler reached for Clint's erection, which was hard and warm against his fingers. Tyler experienced pleasure so intense he wouldn't be able to last much longer. He managed to continue stroking Clint, even as a long shudder eddied its way through his body.

"That's it," Clint urged. "Come for me, Ty."

Tyler let go, his cock milked by the tight ring of muscle as Clint lifted and lowered himself in a steady, perfect rhythm. He tightened his grip on Clint's cock, pumping it only a few times before Clint groaned and jerked against him, the hot, silky ejaculate erupting and spilling down his fingers. A few drops landed just beside his mouth. He tasted its salty sweetness with the tip of his tongue and smiled.

Clint lifted himself from Tyler and fell beside him, pulling him into his arms. They lay quietly a while, tangled together as their heartbeats slowed and their breathing eased back to normal.

I'm in love with you.

The words reverberated again in Tyler's head in Clint's deep rasping voice, as if he were saying them aloud once again. Tyler had heard those words before. He'd even uttered them himself once or twice, though he'd never really believed them, not from the other guy or his own lips.

But this felt different. Clint's words had shot past his brain, zinging like an arrow straight to his heart. Screwing up his courage, Tyler began, "Clint, I think I..." He hesitated, turning to face him.

But Clint's eyes were closed, his breathing deep and even. Tyler watched him a long while, memorizing the curves and planes of his weather-beaten face, his heart actually aching with tenderness. Finally he finished the sentence, his voice little more than a whisper. "...love you too." But Clint, fast asleep, didn't hear.

Chapter 12

They were lying in bed in an easy tangle of limbs as the first streaks of sunlight crept over the sill. Tyler lay quiet, fighting a silent battle in his head. He wanted to tell Clint. He longed to tell him, and yet he couldn't seem to muster the courage. He ached to whisper his secrets about the dark place in his head that made his heart beat too fast and his breath catch in his throat and his mouth run dry. To show Clint what was hidden in the bottom drawer of the nightstand that he'd never shown another soul.

Would Clint understand? Could anyone understand his need, a need so great he'd allowed Wayne to do what he'd done, though the shame of it haunted him still?

"What's got into you, Ty? You've gone rigid as a board."

"I'm sorry," Tyler said, pulling away from Clint's embrace. "I thought you were sleeping. Did I wake you?"

"Nah. Just lyin' here thinkin' how good it feels to be with you."

Tyler smiled in the half-light. "Clint," he said quietly. "There's something..." He paused, his courage ebbing.

"What is it, Ty? What's goin' on in that head of yours?"

"It's just. I was thinking..." Again he paused.

"Go on," Clint urged gently.

"Well, remember last night you said that thing about our special kind of loving not being about abuse, but…"

"That's right."

"But I, well…I need…I mean…" Tyler let out an angry puff of breath. Clint had assured him over and over that he could trust him—he was safe to say whatever was in his mind and heart, so why was this so hard?

"You've got somethin' to say but you're scared to say it," Clint said, as usual honing right in on what was bothering Tyler.

"Yeah," he admitted. "Something bad."

"Bad?"

"Well, I mean, something about me. That I don't think you really understand. Something that might…change things."

Clint pulled himself up against the headboard and faced Tyler with a solemn expression. "Tyler, I can't think of anything at all about you that I might discover that would change how I feel about you." He reached out, touching Tyler's arm. "Listen, I have an idea. Just tell me. Take a deep breath, open your mouth, and just let out whatever it is you got to say. You'll feel a whole lot better after, I promise."

Clint was right. Either he trusted him or he didn't. This was his chance, for the first time in his life, to share what he had kept hidden from everyone, even himself in a way, for so long.

Taking that suggested breath, Tyler rolled from the bed and knelt up on the floor beside it. He reached for the bottom drawer and pulled it open. He could feel Clint's eyes on him but he didn't look up.

His heart bumping against his ribs, he pulled open the drawer, feeling toward the back for what he had never showed another soul—until now.

It was a small black leather whip with a filigreed silver handle. The whip was about seven inches long, a small cat-o-nine tails with knotted ends, and the online catalog had described it as ideal for cock and ball torture.

Cock and ball torture. Just the words sent a shiver of dark lust through Tyler's blood.

Hoping his hand wasn't shaking, Tyler held the whip out to Clint, still not quite able to meet his eye. He could feel the flush of his embarrassment at war with the burn of his desire.

Clint took the whip from his hand. "Nice," he said, drawing out the word as he ran his fingers over the leather falls. "You bought this for yourself?"

Tyler nodded, biting his lip.

"Anyone ever use it on you?"

Slowly Tyler shook his head. He wouldn't have dreamed of showing any of the casual pickups he brought back to the apartment from time to time what he had hidden in the back of his drawer.

Why had he showed Clint? Now Clint would see how twisted he really was. It was one thing to make use of the crops and quirts already available in the tack rooms, and the rope that was handy on any ranch. But it was quite another thing to specifically go out and buy something like that. He wasn't merely submitting to another man's control. By purchasing the whip, he was admitting that he longed for the sensual pain those knotted strands of leather could give him. And now Clint knew it too.

"Tell me what you want, Ty," Clint said softly. "What do you want me to do with this whip?"

"I want…" Tyler's voice came out hoarse. He coughed and cleared his throat. *Please God, let him understand*, Tyler silently prayed. Could anyone understand this unnatural longing?

"Tell me."

He'd showed him the whip. Clint knew his secret now, so why hold back any longer? Clint would think what he thought. It was time to stand up and admit his deepest feelings, no matter what happened next. And so, Tyler said the words: "Pain. I want you to hurt me, Clint. I want you to use this on me. I need it." His voice broke, "I need it so damn bad."

Hot tears sprang into his eyes, tears of shame, of longing, of relief. There. He had said it aloud. He needed to feel the pain. It wasn't just about submission and giving over control. He needed the pain. And he needed a man like Clint to give it to him.

Clint reached for him, smudging away the tear that had slipped down his cheek. "That's right," he said. "You need the pain. And I need to give it to you. Ain't nothin' wrong with that, Ty. For you and me, it's as natural as breathing. It's a part of who we are. Don't feel no shame for that, Ty. Feel proud that you found the courage to tell me. Feel strong that you're goin' to lie down now and take my whip on your cock and balls. You're goin' to do it for me. You're goin' to do it for you. You're goin' to do it for *us*."

Another tear slipped down Tyler's cheek, as gratitude flooded through him. Clint had understood. He hadn't winced with disgust or recoiled in horror. When Tyler finally met his eye, Clint was smiling at him, that slow, sexy smile that always made Tyler's cock hard.

"Get me some rope, Ty. And a pocketknife."

Tyler stood, glad for something to do, something to ease the powerful tension that had built inside him. He went in search of the coil of clothesline he kept in a kitchen drawer. He retrieved his pocketknife along the way and returned to the bedroom.

Clint slid from the bed and accepted the rope and knife from Tyler. "Lie down on your back, arms and legs extended," he ordered, and Tyler obeyed, his heart booming in his chest.

He watched in silent, intent anticipation as Clint cut the rope into lengths and moved around the bed, sliding the rope beneath the mattress. He brought it up at each corner, using the ends to loop Tyler's wrists and ankles in slipknots.

Clint picked up the whip in one hand. With the other, he ran his fingers lightly over Tyler's outstretched arms, lightly squeezing Tyler's biceps. He let the tresses of the whip glide over Tyler's chest and abdomen. He moved the whip lower, the strands tickling at Tyler's cock and gliding over his balls. In spite of Tyler's fear and nervous anticipation, the touch of leather drew a violent shudder from him, and he swallowed hard, feeling almost faint with lust.

"Tell me again, Ty. I want to hear those words. What do you need?"

"I…" Tyler closed his eyes. "I need you to hurt me. To whip me. Please, Sir."

How many times had he fantasized of this moment, of being tied down to the bed with rope, spread eagle and at his faceless dominant lover's mercy? How many nights, drenched in loneliness, near despair, had he fallen asleep dreaming of this very thing? And now that lover had a face, and a name. Clint Darrow was offering him his deepest held secret fantasy, without censure, without judgment, without shame.

It was happening. It was really happening.

~*~

"We'll start easy," Clint said, as he slid the leather over Tyler's thighs, teasing in a circle around his cock and balls without actually touching them. Tyler's eyes were fastened on the whip and again he licked his lips. Clint could feel his nervous anticipation, and beneath it the nearly desperate desire for what Clint was offering. But the guy was as skittish as a wild colt his first time under a saddle.

He understood the courage it must have taken to say those words aloud. And the trust he'd placed in Clint to say them. He sat beside Tyler and stroked his brow with a gentling touch.

"It's okay, Ty. You're safe. Somethin' tells me you've been waitin' a long time for this, and you're ready now. It's time. And I'm the man to take you where you need to go."

Tyler relaxed some against the mattress. Clint reached for Tyler's balls, gently cupping them as he moved the knotted leather over his cock.

Tyler closed his eyes.

"You want it, Ty? You ready?"

Eyes still closed, Tyler whispered, "Yeah," his chest rising and falling as his breath quickened.

Clint let go of Tyler's balls and flicked his wrist, delivering a light, steady rain of leather over Tyler's thighs, cock and balls. Tyler shuddered and gasped, his cock actually straining toward the leather stroke.

Clint watched his face, saw the yearning and the raw desire there. Yes, Tyler was born for this, and Clint was born to give it to him. If pressed he wouldn't have been able to properly explain the sharp, focused thrill that taking someone like Tyler to the edge of their endurance gave him. All he knew was that, just like Tyler, this was exactly where he needed to be.

He flicked the whip with more force, the knotted ends hitting their target with a whoosh of sound. "Ah," Tyler cried, and Clint saw the small red marks the knots had left appearing on his rigid shaft. He struck lower, catching the sensitive skin of Tyler's scrotum. Tyler jerked hard at the ropes that bound his wrists and cried out again.

Clint struck him again, and again, each blow as hard or harder than the last. His own cock was throbbing, his heart racing with excitement as he watched Tyler writhe and heard his sweet, breathy moans and cries. Tyler's cock and balls were reddening from the relentless, stinging kiss of knotted leather. A sheen of sweat had broken out over his skin, the tufts of blond hair beneath his arms darkening and curling.

Clint varied the pace and intensity of the lashing, moving the whip in a dance of unpredictable strokes over Tyler's cock, balls and thighs. Tyler was panting now, his hips rising to meet each stroke.

"Oh god," he cried, as Clint whipped him to a frenzy. "Fuck."

Cords were straining at his neck, his lips parted, his chest heaving. Clint hit him harder, drawing a long, low moan that was as much pleasure as pain. "That's it," Clint urged. "Do it. Come from the whipping. Show me how much you need this."

Sudden, short bursts of pearly ejaculate shot over Tyler's stomach and chest. Clint lowered the whip, watching the passion play of his lover's orgasm, deeply moved to know he had taken him there.

When Clint released him from the rope, Tyler scrambled up, pushing Clint back against the bed with surprising force. For a split second Clint thought he was going to hit him, but instead Tyler crouched between Clint's thighs, reaching with hands and mouth for Clint's cock.

His attentions were nothing short of worship as he took Clint's shaft deep in his throat and then let it go, only to cover it with kisses and long, slow licks of his tongue. He was moving his lips between kisses, and to Clint it looked like he was praying. He focused on Tyler's mouth, trying to see what he was saying, because he heard no sound but his own groans of pleasure.

"Thank you," Tyler whispered. "Thank you, thank you, thank you."

~*~

Clint awoke to the aroma of brewing coffee. He glanced at the bed beside him, which was empty. He stretched lazily and put his hands behind his head. Though he loved being with Ty, he missed the ranch already. He was in no hurry to return, however, having cleared the week with Joe, who owed him about a year of untaken vacation time.

The aching weight of despair Clint had allowed to settle over him the week before had lifted, and in a way that suffering had made this reunion all the sweeter. It had brought into sharp relief how much this mattered. He had nearly let hurt feelings and wounded pride cost him a second chance. If Jonas hadn't kicked some sense into him, he might still be sitting beside that stream, surrounded by pointed sticks like a fence that kept out everything good.

He looked around the bedroom, with its sparse furniture and empty walls. He tried to imagine what it would be like living here all the time. Austin was close enough to real country that within an hour's drive he could lose himself in the rolling hills that surrounded it, but there was no getting around the fact that Austin was the city, and it had enough concrete and glass to last him a lifetime. Sure, there were parks and greenery, but none of the wide open spaces that Clint needed to feel free and easy.

And yet, Tyler was here. Tyler had chosen to make his life here, and Clint loved Tyler. With the whipping, they'd crossed a new line. Tyler had sloughed off his shame like an old skin, no longer needed. There had been fierce, passionate joy in Tyler's grateful thanks afterward. Clint understood Tyler wasn't only thanking him for the whipping, but for helping him to break free of a shame he'd carried like shackles probably most of his life.

Clint was grateful too—grateful for the trust Tyler had placed in him by sharing his deepest secrets and opening himself to the possibility of rejection. Clint had tumbled deeper into this new thing called love, and while it was still kind of scary, it was also powerful and sweet, like a strong, fine whiskey. All his life he'd dreamed of a love like this, though truth to tell, he'd come to believe it only existed in song lyrics and love poems. At least for him, love seemed to have passed him by. Until now.

His musings were interrupted by Tyler, who entered the bedroom carrying two mugs of coffee.

"'Bout time you woke up, sleepyhead." Tyler was wearing only a pair of boxers, his blond hair tousled and falling into his eyes. Clint drank in the sight of him, wondering if he'd ever get tired of Tyler's look of adoration and his boyish, eager longing. He knew he would not.

Tyler settled on the edge of the bed and handed Clint a mug. Clint sat up against the headboard and sipped.

Tyler's cell phone rang and he rummaged on the floor until he found his jeans from last night and pulled it out, glancing at the screen. "It's my sister. I'll just be a sec."

"Hey, what's up?" Tyler said into the phone as he settled on the bed beside Clint. Clint felt Tyler's body go rigid. "Oh, no. Is he okay? How'd it happen?" There was a lengthy pause and then, "You know I can't do that, Sarah. I got this job and all…" Another pause and then, "Yeah, I understand you got a ranch to run. I know…Okay. Okay, I'll figure something out. Let me call you back this afternoon, okay? I'm barely awake."

There was another long pause, during which Tyler looked toward Clint, shrugging his shoulders in a gesture of apology before turning away again. "Okay, okay," he finally said. "Look, I'll call you back this afternoon, I promise. Just give me a little time here. "

He ended the call and stood staring at the counter, seemingly lost in thought.

"What happened? What's going on?" Clint asked.

Tyler looked up. "My dad. He fell off a horse this morning and broke his leg. That was Sarah, calling from the hospital. They're going to bring him home, but he's gonna be laid up a while. They expect me to just drop everything and come help run the place."

Clint nodded. "Makes sense. You're family. You know the business. But then, you've got this new career now."

Tyler frowned. "Yeah. I got this job. But it's more than that. She doesn't understand. I can't go back. I never told her..." Tyler stopped himself mid-sentence. He reached for his mug and Clint had the feeling he was hiding behind it.

Clint sipped his coffee and then ventured, "Maybe you can just go back a week or two, till they can hire someone?"

Tyler stiffened and sat upright. "I can't go back." He stated the words flatly, as if there were no other possible option.

"Why not, Ty? Don't you think they'd give you a leave of absence for a family emergency?"

Tyler looked blank for a moment. Then he said, "Oh, you mean the magazine? Nah, it's not that. To tell you the truth, I'm not even sure that's what I want to do. I miss the horses something awful. Being in the country last week really brought that home to me. I miss the ranch. I miss riding. I miss the night sounds that don't include honking horns. I miss my family."

"Then what is it keepin' you away? They want you back. You want to go back. Seems pretty simple to me."

Tyler shook his head miserably. "Nothing's simple anymore. Not since I fucked everything up."

Suddenly Clint understood. "It's that guy Wayne, ain't it? The jerk who abused your trust? He was back at your ranch, wasn't he? Still there, I take it? You gonna let him win by stayin' away?"

"It's not that simple," Tyler replied.

"Okay. So tell me. What's so complicated?"

"It wasn't like with you, Clint. Lord, I'm ashamed to admit this to you, to anyone, but I guess you deserve to know it." His expression was anguished. "I let him treat me like a piece of shit. I let him call me a faggot and laugh in my face when I protested. I got off on the rough sex we had, and the dirty things he said when he was whipping my ass or had me trussed up like a calf, his dick down my throat and a sneer on his face. I knew it was sick and shameful, but I—I needed…" His voice trailed to a whisper, "… I needed the pain."

Clint reached for Tyler, drawing him into his arms. Tyler hid his face on Clint's shoulder and Clint stroked his hair. "You need the pain but only when it's given with love and received with courage. He exploited that need, Tyler. He was a bully who took advantage of you, pure and simple. He's the one who should be ashamed, not you."

"It's worse than that," Tyler murmured. "He started demanding things. He wanted me to get my father to promote him to foreman. He threatened me that if I didn't do what he wanted, he'd tell my family what we were doing. He would have been out of a job, but I would have lost everything." Tyler pulled away from Clint and dropped his head into his hands.

"Ty, listen to me," Clint entreated. "Wayne twisted what should be sacred between two people. He corrupted the gift you offered him. Then he tried to blackmail you into doin' what he wanted. I can understand why you felt you had no way out. But maybe there's a way back in, if you're ready to go home again."

His face still hidden, Tyler shook his head. "I can't. I just can't."

Clint thought about this. He understood he couldn't force Tyler to do the right thing, or anything at all. It was up to Tyler to make that kind of decision on his own. Clint understood too he didn't know all the details of the situation or what Tyler was really facing.

All Clint knew for sure was that he wanted this man in his life, on whatever terms Tyler was ready or willing to give him. Clint closed his eyes, aware he had just made a decision. "Ty, I got something to say."

He waited until Tyler looked up, and then he waited a beat longer.

"I love you. I understand that now, better than I've ever understood a blessed thing in this life. I know you ain't perfect. Me neither, trust me. We're feelin' our way together in this thing, but that's the key—together. We're forgin' trust and understandin', so I hope you can hear this in the way it's intended."

He reached for Tyler, putting his arm around his shoulder. "Ty, it seems to me you've spent your life runnin'. Runnin' from your own feelin's, runnin' from a man who did you wrong, runnin' from your family instead lettin' them in, trustin' them enough to understand who you really are. Even runnin' from me."

Tyler opened his mouth but Clint held up his hand. "Just hear me out. I've spent a fair portion of my life runnin' too. Runnin' from feelings that might get me hurt. Now I'm fixin' to turn forty and damn it, I'm done runnin'. I found what I'm lookin' for, and that's you, Ty. I came here to win you back, and I'm tellin' you now, I ain't leavin' you, not unless you tell me to go. If you're not ready to head back home, that's a decision only you can make. But I've come to a decision of my own. I'm ready to leave the ranch, Tyler. I'm ready to uproot myself and move to Austin, if it means I can be with you."

He watched the stunned surprise move over Tyler's face. Clint pushed on. "I figured out something this past week, sittin' by the creek and thinkin' 'bout my life, and 'bout things like what really matters in this world. The way I see it, there's two things that matter—love and family. I got no family left, Ty. But I got love. For the first time in my life, I found a man I can love. I ain't gonna let that pass me by. Not this time."

Clint's voice caught and he swallowed, caught by surprise by the sudden tears pressing just behind his eyes. He let out a breath and then shut his mouth. He'd said what he had to say.

~*~

Tyler saw Clint's dark eyes flood with the tears and he turned sharply away, wrapping his arms around his chest as he tried to compose himself and his thoughts. Were his ears playing tricks, or did Clint Darrow, a diehard born-and-bred cowboy just say he'd uproot himself and move to the city? Could Clint really leave the wide open country he loved just to be with him?

This declaration penetrated Tyler's mind and heart in a more powerful way than any pretty words or even the most intense lovemaking ever could. *He loves me,* he thought, and it was the first time in his life he really knew such a thing for sure.

But when he turned around, Clint was nowhere to be seen. The bedroom door was shut and Tyler had the sudden horrible realization that Clint had misunderstood his action—thinking Tyler was turning his back as a rejection.

He leaped toward the door and wrenched it open. He couldn't let Clint get away. He had to set things to right. Frantically he scanned the living room, but it was empty.

"Clint," he cried, racing toward the front door. It was then he noticed the sliding patio door was open. He hurried toward it and stepped out onto the concrete pad. Clint was there, leaning against the flimsy iron railing, his back toward Tyler as he faced the parking lot.

Tyler moved beside him, longing to pull Clint into his arms, but sensing a certain reserve that held him back. So instead he moved to stand beside him, leaning his arms on the railing beside Clint, their shoulders touching.

They stood silently side by side for a minute or so. Then Tyler reached out, putting his hand on Clint's arm. Clint looked slowly toward him, his expression difficult to read.

"I was scared you'd left, Clint. I don't want you to go. Not ever. I guess I was just so floored when you said you'd give up ranch life, just to be with me. I—I didn't know how to respond."

Clint put his hand over Tyler's and shook his head, a small smile on his lips. "Not *just*, Ty. If I've finally learned something from all this, it's that love is what matters. It's what makes life worth living."

Tyler let the wonder he was feeling seep into his voice as he finally put it into words. "So then, you must...really love me."

Clint laughed and punched Tyler in the shoulder. "You're figurin' that out, huh? Takin' you a while, boy."

Tyler grinned sheepishly and ducked his head, but then the smile slid away from his face. He took a deep breath and let it out slowly. "I got something to say, Clint. It hit me in the gut when I thought for a minute you'd gone. I don't even want to be here. Austin isn't my home. I've just been hiding out here. Running, just like you said. I miss the ranch. I miss the horses and my family. I can't even imagine you here in this big city. You would be liked a penned calf here, Clint. You'd go stir crazy in a week."

"I'd be fine," Clint asserted.

Tyler shook his head. "I doubt it. But the fact that you'd do it. That you're willing to make that kind of sacrifice for me..." Again he shook his head in wonder. "This whole journalism thing—it was just a cover, something to hide behind. I guess I thought if I ran far enough, I could run from my own feelings."

He hit the railing with his fist. "I know what I need to do, Clint. I guess I've known all along but I just wasn't ready to face it. I have to go back. I have to do the right thing by my family. But more importantly, I have to do the right thing for myself."

Clint was watching him, waiting. Tyler took a breath and then he said it: "I have to face Wayne Hurley. I have to let him know what he did wasn't okay."

Clint nodded. "Let's go inside."

They moved together back into the apartment. Clint took Tyler into his arms and it felt so good just to be there. "I'm proud of you, Ty. It takes a real man to face up to his own fears."

They held each other for a long time, as the words Tyler longed to say moved slowly through him. And then, for the first time in his life he found the courage to say the words he meant with all his heart.

"I love you."

Chapter 13

Tyler pulled out his cell phone when they were about a mile from the Double S Ranch. "Hey, Sarah. We should be there in a few minutes."

"We?"

Tyler had called her back once he'd made the decision to return to the ranch. He'd only packed enough to stay a week or so, but in his heart he recognized he was coming home. He'd called his editor to let her know he had a family emergency and needed to take a leave of absence.

Clint had offered to drive him home in his truck and Tyler had readily agreed. They could get his car later, when he figured things out.

"Yeah. My friend, Clint Darrow, is with me. I guess I should have mentioned that when we spoke yesterday."

"No, that's fine. Any friend of yours is welcome, Tyler. Mama and Dad are thrilled you're coming home. Well," she paused, "Mama is, anyway. Dad'll come around though, you'll see, now that the prodigal son is finally returning."

Tyler groaned. Sarah was three years Tyler's senior. Their father had kept it no secret that his firstborn was supposed to have been a son, though over the years he could never fault Sarah for her dedication to the ranch and pure love of the horses.

When Tyler was born however, after his mother had sustained two miscarriages, his father's jubilation had become part of the family lore. He finally had a son. The second S in the Double S Ranch, he'd told Tyler more times than he could count, stood for son—Sutton and Son.

"But Sarah's the one who wants to run the place," Tyler had protested when he was small. "Sarah should be the second S." This too had become part of the family lore, though not surprisingly, Sarah was less than amused by it all, angrily insisting that girls could do as much as boys, and do it better.

In time her father had had no choice but to agree, as Sarah dedicated her life to the horses, and even ended up marrying their foreman, Bert Carlson. But still Tom Sutton held firm to the idea that Tyler would be the one to ultimately take over the place, once he was gone. This had rankled Sarah to no end, and at the same time, put unwelcome pressure on Tyler. For though he also loved the horses and the ranching way of life, he resented his father's foregone assumption that he had no choice in the matter.

As they pulled up the long drive that led to the main house, Sarah came running out the front door of the house. She was still in her leather vest and chaps, her long blond hair pulled back in a ponytail, and Tyler knew she had just come from riding. Sarah loved those horses more than she loved Bert, or so it seemed to Tyler.

Clint and Tyler climbed down from the truck and introductions were made. "Let's go on back to your place and put your stuff down," Sarah suggested, as Clint and Tyler hoisted their duffel bags over their shoulders. "I got your cabin all aired out this morning. We've kept it empty all this time, though a couple of the hands wanted to take it over. I just *knew* you'd be back."

Over initial protests by Tyler's mother, Tyler, while not moving off the property altogether, had insisted on having his own space after college. He had taken over the cabin once occupied by Bert, before he'd married the boss's daughter and moved into the big house.

Sarah smiled warmly at Tyler and he realized just how much he'd missed her. They walked along the path behind the house in the direction of the bunkhouse and Tyler's cabin. "Dad's napping and Mama's washing up from lunch, so we got time," she informed him.

"Good," Tyler replied. "Because I got something to tell you before we go up to the house. Something I should have told you a long time ago."

Sarah, who had moved a little ahead of them on the path, looked back, her arched eyebrows raised. "Sounds important. Is this where I find out I was adopted and am really the daughter of the Enchanted Horse Queen?"

Tyler laughed and turned to Clint. "When I was a little kid, I had nightmares sometimes, and I would go to Sarah's room and climb into her bed. She would make up these great stories that usually featured the Enchanted Horse Queen, this magical creature who was human by day, but horse by night, with a coat of real silver and hooves with diamond shoes."

"Sounds right poetic," Clint remarked with a smile.

"Clint's a cowboy poet," Tyler told Sarah. "I met him when I was covering a cowboy poetry festival for the magazine." They talked about that for a few minutes as they entered the cabin and put their things down. It was a one-room affair not unlike Clint's place, though Tyler's included a loft above that served as his bedroom. Tyler glanced upward, imagining Clint sleeping in his bed and it reminded him of his resolve.

"I even stocked your refrigerator," Sarah remarked. "Lone Star Beer and Dr. Pepper."

"I'm gonna like this girl." Clint beamed and Tyler laughed.

Tyler got them each a can of soda and said, "Sit down, Sarah. I was serious when I said I had something I want to talk to you about."

"I think I'm just gonna step out and take a little walk—" Clint began.

"No," Tyler said quickly. "Please, stay. I want you here, Clint. If that's okay." Clint nodded and the three of them sat down, Tyler beside Sarah on the futon couch, Clint opposite them on one of the two chairs that faced the couch.

Tyler cupped his hands around his soda, suddenly wishing it were a beer, though the courage he needed to draw on now couldn't be gotten from a bottle. They'd discussed it at length during the four-hour drive from Austin, and Tyler, with Clint's love behind him, had been more than ready to finally tell his family he was gay and proud of it. But now that he was sitting here beside his sister, the words didn't come so easy.

Sarah turned expectantly toward Tyler. "Okay, little brother. What're you so all-fired up to tell me? I'm all ears."

"Well, I…" Tyler paused, the carefully planned speech he'd written in his head now completely inaccessible. Sarah was watching him with a kind smile. He glanced nervously toward Clint, who gave him an imperceptible encouraging nod, as if to say, *you can do it*.

"You know how Mama was always after me to marry and raise a family. And how I always put her off with stuff like I was too young, and someday I'd settle down."

"Uh huh." Sarah nodded.

"Well." Tyler took a breath and forged on. "The reason I never dated much in high school and never brought any girl home to meet the folks is…" The air felt close in the cabin and Tyler pulled at the neck of his T-shirt, suddenly overly-warm. Both Sarah and Clint were watching him expectantly. Feeling like he used to as a kid when he'd be poised high up on the ledge of the old rock, ready to dive into the lake they called the mud hole, Tyler took the leap.

"I'm gay, Sarah. And Clint here's more than my friend. A lot more."

Though if anyone in the family would understand, it was Sarah, he still half-expected her to scream, or leap up in horror and run from the cabin. What she did surprised him even more.

She laid her hand lightly on his arm and smiled. "I know that, hon. I've known it for years. But I'm honored you finally found the trust to confide in me. That means a lot."

Tyler stared at his sister, his mouth falling open. She shook her head and started to laugh. Clint began to laugh too. After a moment, Tyler joined in.

If only it would be so easy to tell his father. But that, Tyler knew, would be no laughing matter.

"Well, I guess if it took breaking my leg to get you to come home, then it was worth it. Now what do I have to do to get you to stay? Have a heart attack?"

"Dad, cut it out." For some reason, no matter how many years passed, whenever Tyler got around his father, he felt like he was fourteen.

Tyler sat beside his father in the master suite of the sprawling ranch house where he'd grown up. Tom Sutton, a large man with light brown hair sprinkled liberally with gray, lay propped against many pillows on the king-size bed, his left leg in a long white cast that went from thigh to ankle.

"I'm sorry it's been so long," Ty replied. "I would have come sooner, but with work and all..."

"What, writing little stories for some frou-frou magazine is called work now? Last I looked, work was usin' your back and your hands to earn an honest livin'. Sittin' at some desk in some air-conditioned office ain't *work*. Not for a Sutton, at any rate. Not when there's real work to be done on the ranch and not enough good men to do it."

Tyler's neck heated. He bit down a scathing retort, reminding himself his dad was laid up and no doubt frustrated and in pain. "Dad," he tried, "That's not fair. I—"

"Oh, save me your excuses." Tom Sutton snorted. "I should just be glad you finally came home. I guess every man needs a little time to sow their wild oats." He squinted suddenly at Tyler. "Did you sow some, boy? Is that what all this nonsense was about, you takin' off like someone had lit a fire under your butt? Have you got a little filly in the wings you ain't tellin' us about? Is that what took you gallavantin' off to Austin? Is your mama finally gonna get to hear them dang weddin' bells she's always goin' on about?"

"Jesus, Dad, don't start with that—" Tyler began.

"Okay, okay. But answer the question. You finally got a girl at least?"

Was this his chance? His father had offered the opening by asking if there was someone in his life. Was now the time to finally tell the truth, a truth he'd been hiding for so many years? Would his father be able to understand? To accept him for who he was?

"Dad, I—"

"Knock, knock," came a singsong voice. Tyler's mother, a small woman with fading blond hair and a ready smile, poked her head into the room. She had greeted Tyler with hugs and kisses when he'd entered the house, without one word of recrimination. That, Tyler had known, was waiting upstairs.

"Sorry to interrupt you boys, but Dr. Bradley was nice enough to stop by, Tom. He just wants to pop up and see how you're doing. Isn't that thoughtful?"

"Doctors make house calls in Austin, boy?" Tom barked. Replying to his own question, he added, "I doubt it." Turning to his wife, he said, "Sure, send him up. That's right nice of him to stop by."

"I'll check in later," Tyler said, frustration and relief coursing through him in equal measure. There would be time, plenty of time, to set things right with his parents. How they chose to react would be their responsibility and their problem, not his.

His parents occupied with the doctor, Tyler made his way to the stables, eager to see his horses at last, especially Star, his pride and joy. Star had foaled that spring, and he'd missed it, though Sarah had kept him apprised of the birth and sent pictures of the proud mama and her new colt, which Sarah had named Midnight because of his coal black coat.

Sarah had already taken Clint to see the horses, as they all agreed Clint should be introduced to Tom and Linda Sutton later, at supper, when things had settled down a bit.

Tyler entered the stalls where Star was kept. It was empty and he realized she must be in the pasture with her baby, enjoying the late afternoon sun. He was just about to go out in search of them when he heard a voice that made his blood run hot and cold at the same time.

"Well, look who finally came back home with his tail between his legs."

Tyler turned around to see Wayne Hurley leaning against the doorframe, his cowboy hat tilted at an angle that hid his eyes, a cruel smile lifting the edges of his mouth. Wayne was movie star handsome, with thick, curling brown hair, hazel eyes flecked with gold, his jaw square, his lips full and lush.

Tyler knew he had to face Wayne straight out of the chute, but he'd planned to seek him out, not the other way around. He'd been rehearsing that speech too in his head on and on the way to the ranch, determined at last to have his say and put Wayne firmly in his place. But, now, as he stared at Wayne, all thoughts and rehearsed speeches flew from his head.

Those eyes, which used to hold Tyler in such thrall, burning into him with what Tyler used to think was passion, now seemed cold and flat, neither giving nor reflecting light, like a reptile. Wayne spoke in a slow, derisive drawl. "Well, if it ain't my personal piece of ass, finally come sniveling back to make his amends. Bet ya' missed me, didn't ya', boy? Ain't nobody around. Get on your knees and show me just how much you missed me."

"I'm done with all that, Wayne," Tyler snapped, his voice low as he struggled to contain his anger and the lingering shame beneath it. "You got no hold over me. Not anymore."

Wayne moved closer. He had been with the horses and he was dusty and sweaty, the smell pungent as he approached. His laugh was low and cruel. "I got no hold? You think just 'cause you ran away that I don't still own you? I knew you'd be back." He moved closer, too close for comfort and Tyler stepped back. "And it's about time, too," Wayne continued, "'cause I been lookin' for a whippin' boy, and my dick is in need of attention."

The anger bubbled over, obliterating any lingering shame. Tyler understood now, on a gut level, that what Wayne had offered—no, what Wayne had *taken*—had nothing to do with what Tyler really needed or craved. It was as far from what he shared with Clint as a wooden nickel was compared to a coin of solid gold.

In a sudden movement he lunged toward Wayne, pushing him hard against the wall of the stall as he grabbed a handful of Wayne's shirt and twisted it in his fist. "I just told you, I ain't interested in what you got to offer. So I'd thank you to keep your dirty mouth shut and your filthy thoughts to yourself."

Wayne wrenched himself from Tyler's grip and Tyler let go, clenching his hands into fists at his sides. He hadn't meant to lose his temper. He'd intended to freeze Wayne with haughty indifference. Now he breathed hard through his nose, willing himself to calm down.

Wayne smoothed down his shirt. There was a spot of red on each cheek and Tyler knew he was angry, and no doubt surprised to find the change in the once-passive Tyler. He grinned, a slow, unpleasant grimace as his eyes narrowed. "What happened to you in Austin, boy? Did your mind turn to mush? Did you forget you're nothin' but a snivelin' faggot who gets off on being fucked up the ass and whupped till you bleed?"

Tyler imagined smashing his fist into that perfect, square jaw, but he kept his arms at his sides. "I haven't forgotten a thing. I haven't forgotten that you threatened me with blackmail. You're not worth the horse shit on the bottom of my boot. You try to mess with me, and I'll give it back, just watch. I can give as good as I get."

Wayne laughed, the sound harsh, though Tyler could sense a slight faltering in his cocky self-assurance. "You forget, Ty. I know your secrets. You better have your dad make me foreman, or I'll spill 'em all."

"And I know yours, too, you fool. So I'd advise you to keep your mouth shut, if you know what's good for you," Tyler snapped.

"Oh, yeah?" Wayne blustered. "Well, I want you to kneel down and open yours." He smirked, cupping his balls and licking his lips.

Tyler wanted nothing so much as to take a good swing at the guy, but he held himself in check. Wayne Hurley was so not worth it. "You're an ass, Wayne," Tyler said, shaking his head. "You're good with the horses, which is the only reason you haven't been fired. You'll never make foreman. You have to have brains for that job, and when the lord was handing them out, he shorted you, I'm afraid."

Wayne pursed his lips and squinted, and Tyler could tell he was trying to come up with a snappy response, but it wasn't quite working out. Clearly he had been thrown by Tyler's new attitude toward him. He'd obviously expected to pick up where they'd left off. Tyler only wished he'd come to his senses six months ago, instead of just running.

Though he knew he shouldn't even waste his breath, Tyler added, "You know what, Wayne? When I left, I was running away, not from you so much as my own shame. I'm a different man now. I've learned that my feelings and needs are nothing to be ashamed of. I'm proud of who and what I am. And nobody, not even a closeted, in-denial, bullying, sadistic son of a bitch like you can take that away from me."

Wayne moved close again, the stink of his sweat ripe in Tyler's nostrils. "You little shit," he snarled in a low voice. "I ain't gay. How many times I got to tell you, *you're* the one who takes it up the ass, not me. You're the faggot."

Tyler shook his head, giving up. "Wayne, you are such an asshole." He walked toward the paddock. Turning back, he said, "One last thing. Watch your step around me. This is the Double S Ranch, and in case you hadn't noticed, my name is Sutton too."

Tyler saw Star and her colt in the pasture, and while he longed to go see her and greet the newest addition to the ranch, he needed to seize the moment, while his resolve remained strong. He caught up briefly with Clint and Sarah, who were leaning on the fence watching the horses in the pasture, and let them know he had some business to finish back at the house.

He'd told Wayne he was proud of who and what he was. Well, it was time to put his money where his mouth was. He'd come home and now it was time to stand up to his father, man to man.

He could hear his mother humming in the kitchen, no doubt

preparing a feast to celebrate his return, but he didn't stop to check. He took the stairs two at a time, glad in a way his dad was laid up, since Tom Sutton was always in motion when working the ranch, with only half an ear available for anyone who tried to talk to him.

He approached the master bedroom and took a deep breath, tucking his shirt in and pushing his fingers through his hair as he moved toward the door, which was ajar. "Dad?" He looked into the room. Tom Sutton was awake, the remote control in his hand, his eyes on the TV.

He turned toward Tyler. "I don't know why I pay for that damn satellite dish. Now instead of three channels of nothin', there's a hundred channels of nothin'." He clicked off the TV with a snort of disgust and turned to Tyler, his eyebrows raised.

"What did the doctor have to say?" Tyler asked, as he settled into a chair nearby.

"Six weeks. Like I have time to be laid up for six whole weeks. And the doc has me on all these dang pain meds. Can't hardly think straight. I got work to do—no time for this crap." He glowered a moment at Tyler, as if it were his fault he was laid up. "At least you're finally back and can start pullin' your weight again. I got accounts to settle and some sales to negotiate. You can put some of that fancy book learnin' of yours to use and get to work on them accounts."

"I'd be happy to, Dad. But first we need to talk. I got something to say to you."

His father regarded him. "That right? You gonna explain the real reason you skedaddled?"

Tyler counted to five slowly in his head. This wasn't going to be easy, but then, he hadn't expected it to be. "In a way, yes," he replied. "When I left here six months ago, I was still a boy. I hadn't faced up to some important issues in my life. Or more precisely, I hadn't been honest with you and Mama about some things. I've learned a lot these past months away, and one thing I learned is that I don't need to be ashamed of who and what I am."

He sat up straighter, squaring his shoulders. "I'm gay. I've known it for sure since I was fourteen. I've hidden it all this time because I knew, or thought I knew, the reception I'd get from family and friends. I was afraid of being ostracized and rejected just for being myself, so I tried to be someone else. I'm done with all that. I'm proud of who and what I am. I'm done hiding the truth from you or anyone else."

He closed his mouth and waited, watching the high color seep over his father's beefy face. Tom Sutton opened and closed his mouth several times, like a fish caught on a hook, but no sound came. Finally he spluttered, "Gay? As in a homo sexual?" He said the word as if it were two words. "A queer?"

Tyler snorted, a grim smile moving over his face. "All of the above. Lots of other terms I'm sure you could come up with, but yeah. That's about the size of it. I'm still the same man. I can still run a ranch, ride a horse, balance the books and love my family. But I'm no longer willing to keep this basic part of me a secret any longer."

His father was nodding slowly, and Tyler forced himself to remain calm. He'd said his piece. Now it was up to his father what he did with it. Tyler found himself fully ready to accept the consequences. One thing he'd learned in Austin, there was more to the world than just horse ranching, and for that matter, more than one ranch in Texas. He had skills and he had options. If his father couldn't accept him on his own terms, he'd carve out a new life on his own.

"Makes sense," his father finally said. "Your mama always fretted how you never seemed to like any one girl. With Sarah goin' on thirty-three now and still no babies, she took to puttin' all her apples in your basket, if you follow me."

Tyler nodded, well aware of his mother's earnest desire for grandchildren.

"I knew you were hidin' something," his father continued. "When you put up the fuss about movin' out of the family home, I should have known it was about more than just tryin' to assert your independence. You needed a place to bring them boys—"

"Stop it." Tyler held up his hand in warning and to his surprise, his father shut up. "This isn't about my private life. It's about who I am. Now you can accept me on my terms, or not. That's up to you. I'm being honest with you—talking to you man to man. I would ask that you do the same."

Maybe it was his imagination, but something like respect seemed to move over Tom Sutton's features and he nodded again. "Fair enough." He squinted again toward Tyler. "But you know, it's a strange choice, especially out here deep in the heart of Texas. If you were in New York City, maybe, where anything goes. But out here in God's country…"

"It's not a choice. I didn't wake up one day and decide to be gay. Believe me, much of my youth was spent fervently wishing I wasn't, and doing my best to ignore and deny it. This is who I *am*. If you want to go that route, it's who *God* made me, though I personally don't think he bothers with stuff like that. It's the luck of the draw. I used to think I was unlucky because of it, but I've figured out now, finally, that luck's got nothing to do with it. We take the hand that's dealt us, and it's how we play it that matters."

His father nodded again, and Tyler wondered if he were actually reaching him on some level. He plunged on before losing his nerve. "I've met a good man. A man I really care about, who cares about me. His name is Clint Darrow and he's here. I'm bringing him to supper so you can meet him."

"He's here?" Tom Sutton fairly shouted. "On my ranch? You brought a queer to my ranch?"

Tyler stood, anger coursing through him. What an idiot, to think his narrow-minded, bigoted father would ever understand. But to his surprise, his father lifted both hands, palms up, as if in surrender. "Wait, I'm sorry, son. That was uncalled for. I know this is the twenty-first century, and things are different with this internet business and free love and all that stuff."

In spite himself, Tyler suppressed a grin at his father's naiveté. At least he was actually talking, and hadn't just ordered Tyler summarily from his sight. His father continued. "Listen, son. I know I've been hard on you over the years. That's because you're my only *son*. My boy. I was countin' on you to carry on the line. I guess if I was honest, I always knew there was somethin' funny about you. You know, this, uh, *gay* thing." He said it like it was an affliction, something to be politely ignored, if possible, but Tyler didn't call him on it.

"I shut my eyes because I didn't want to see," he continued. "But for all that, you're still my son, and I love you." Tyler's heart skipped a beat. His father had never, in his memory, said those words to him.

He looked at his father, the large, powerful man who had ruled so much of his life for so many years, and realized, despite all his imperfections, he was a good man who was doing the best he could. "I love you too. And thank you."

Mama was next, but having passed what he considered the toughest hurdle of his father, Tyler was almost lighthearted as he approached his mother in the kitchen. She was standing over the stove, stirring something in a pot that smelled delicious.

She sat him at the table, insisting he have some cookies and lemonade to tide him over before supper, and he didn't protest. "Mama," he said to her back as he chewed a bite of chocolate chip cookie. "I got something to tell you."

And again he shared his secret, the defining secret of his life, tossing away the very last of the chains he had wrapped around himself all these years. His mother came to the table and sat beside him. Like Sarah, she said gently, "I know, Ty. I've always known, in my heart. It ain't somethin' you can hide from your mama."

Now it was Tyler's turn to be surprised. "You knew? But why then all the talk about grandbabies and wedding bells and when would I meet a nice girl?"

His mother looked a little sheepish. She stared down at her hands. "I was savin' face for us both, I guess. Playin' a part, you might say, same as you. I figured you needed to keep it quiet, this bein' West Texas and all, not exactly the most tolerant part of the world." She looked up at Tyler with a grin, acknowledging what an understatement that was. "And then there was your dad."

Of course. Linda Sutton had spent most of her life doing her best to placate and soothe the sometimes fiery-tempered Tom. This was one more way she kept things running smoothly, at least in her mind. Tyler understood, and where this once would have made him angry, now it only made him a little sad. And even that might not be fair—who was he to say how two people managed their lives and their relationship with one another? They'd been married thirty-seven years, so maybe they were doing something right.

"So, you're—you're okay with it?" Tyler finally said.

Linda put her hand over his. "Of course I am, honey. You're my boy. Would I rather you found a nice girl and got married and had kids? I'd be lying if I said otherwise. But we all make our choices in this life, and I can't hardly fault you for yours."

Again the choice thing, but he let it go. "Thanks, Mama. That means a lot to me. More than you know. And I really think you'll like Clint. He came with me. He's with Sarah now, getting an overview of the place. I'm bringing him for supper to meet you all."

"Your father knows this?" she said, looking suddenly alarmed.

"He does," Tyler affirmed. "I talked to him first. He's okay with it. He said I was still his son and he loves me."

His mother smiled. "Of course he does, Tyler. You're the second S in the Double S Ranch."

Chapter 14

Clint felt a bittersweet nostalgia for his own family as he watched everyone take their seats around the table. His family hadn't been especially close, but even so, family was family. But his parents were both dead and his older brother, Daniel, had joined the Army when Clint was sixteen. Daniel had been running then, running from their abusive father, an angry, bitter man who ran their farm into the ground before drinking himself to death when Clint was still in his early twenties.

While Daniel and he still kept in touch by the occasional email, his brother, who had taken the brunt of their father's alcohol-fueled rages, had never come home again. He had settled in Germany, a career military man, and Clint hadn't seen him in over twenty years.

Joe and his wife often had Clint to supper, along with their children and grandchildren, but it wasn't the same as your own flesh and blood. Jonas was as close as he'd had to family all these years. And now there was Tyler. Was it possible he'd known him only a few weeks? Though he cautioned himself that he was still probably in the first flush of new love, he felt deep inside that he'd known Ty forever, and had only been waiting to catch up with him again, at long last.

Tyler sat beside him at the round dinner table. The table was covered in a blue checkered cloth and set with what was probably the family's good china. Tyler looked happy but nervous. On his other side were Sarah and her husband, Bert. Mrs. Sutton was bustling around the kitchen while Mr. Sutton, his leg resting on an extra chair, took up two places, a large mug of beer nearly empty in front of him.

The introductions had gone fairly smoothly, once Tyler and Bert had managed to carry Mr. Sutton down the stairs in a kind of seat made from their joined hands. Mr. Sutton had looked Clint up and down as they shook hands, as if he was hunting for horns or a sign painted on his forehead or some other indicator of his sexual orientation.

"So, Clint," Mr. Sutton now intoned. "Sarah tells me you're a poet. One of them cowboy poets. Your kind is into poetry, I reckon."

Clint raised his eyebrows. "My kind?" He pretended to be confused.

"Oh, well, you know," the flustered Mr. Sutton replied. "Uh, you know," he finished lamely, looking toward Tyler for support, but none was forthcoming. "Kinda hard to make a livin' writin' verse, ain't it?"

"I would imagine so," Clint said drily. "I don't make my livin' at it, though. It's just a hobby. I'm the foreman over at the Ransom Ranch up in Ransom Canyon. Maybe you've heard of it."

Mr. Sutton's mouth dropped open. "Joe Henderson's bull ranch? *That* Ransom Ranch?"

Bert chimed in, "That was your ranch had the prize winning bull at the livestock fair this past year, ain't that right?"

Clint nodded, unable to contain the surge of pride. "Sure is. We got a lot of prize winnin' breeder bulls. In fact, there were some thefts recently of some of our prize semen. Tyler here helped solve the mystery." He looked at Tyler, who smiled.

"I thought you were a journalist in the big city, Ty," Mrs. Sutton remarked as she set a heaping plate of chicken and dumplings, one of Clint's childhood favorites, on the center of the table beside a basket of biscuits and a platter of greens. "How'd you come to be solving mysteries?"

"Investigative journalism," Tyler said, grinning at Clint. "Actually Clint was the one following up on the thefts and I just tagged along. Turned out it was a guy who had no idea of the value of what he was taking. He was just a kid really, in over his head."

Mr. Sutton was apparently still back at the earlier conversation. "You said you're the *foreman*? You've got all that responsibility?" He shook his head in obvious disbelief. "Does he know? Does your boss know…?" Mr. Sutton repeated, apparently having trouble with the concept.

"Dad," Tyler interrupted in a warning tone.

Clint put his hand on Tyler's arm. "It's okay, Ty." He turned to Mr. Sutton, forcing his face into respectful lines, half-amused at the older man's obvious discomfiture. "Does he know what, sir?"

"Well, uh, you know…" Again Mr. Sutton appeared flustered. He took a large bite of his biscuit and wiped the butter that dripped down his chin with his napkin.

"Does he know I'm gay? Is that what you're askin', sir?" Clint kept his tone respectful, and managed to hold back the smile that was trying to break through.

Mr. Sutton flushed, but nodded.

"Why yes, sir, he does. I've worked for him nigh on ten years now, and he's quite satisfied with my performance, at least that's what he tells me. I don't guess it much matters to him what I do in my private life. Most folks where I'm from pretty much keep that sort of thing to themselves." He opened his eyes wide in his best attempt at courteous innocence. "Is it different here at the Double S?"

"Why, no. Uh, no, certainly not," Mr. Sutton said, reaching for his beer mug.

There was silence for a while, save for the clattering of cutlery and clinking of glass. Mrs. Sutton had finally sat down at the table and Clint passed her the biscuits, which she accepted with a smile.

There was a sudden, sharp rapping on the kitchen door. Mrs. Sutton turned toward the sound. "Whoever can that be? The boys know better than to bother us at supper time."

The rapping persisted and then changed to pounding. The voice of a young man could be heard. "I know you're in there, Bert Carlson. Come out and face me like a man." The voice was slurred and Clint would have bet his bottom dollar the guy was drunk. He glanced at Tyler, who had gone suddenly pale, and he knew all at once who it must be at the door.

"Bert," Tyler's father demanded, "What the hell is that about?"

Bert was shaking his head. "That's that damn Wayne Hurley. I gave him some new assignments this afternoon, took him off workin' directly with the horses for a while. He wasn't real happy about it, but truth to tell, this isn't the first time Wayne's hit the bottle a little too hard. I don't want him around the horses right now."

The banging continued. "You can't demote me and get away with it. Not for no queer. I don't care if he is a Sutton." Wayne shouted.

Tyler pushed back his chair abruptly, nearly sending it toppling. Clint reached out a steadying hand. "I'll go see to Wayne," Tyler said. But before he could make his way from the dining room to the kitchen, they could hear the sound of the door opening.

A clearly very drunk young man burst into the dining room, a bottle of whiskey in his hand, blood in his eye. He stumbled a little, then raised his bottle toward Mr. Sutton. "Carlson's tryin' to demote me. He don't know what I know about your boy here."

"Wayne," Tyler began, an urgency in his voice as he moved toward the drunk man. The color that had seeped away a moment before now edged up his neck and cheeks. "You're drunk. Get out of here."

"I may be drunk," Wayne slurred, taking a swig from his bottle for emphasis, "but that don't change the facts. Ain't nobody gonna demote me for some queer." He turned again toward Mr. Sutton. "Your boy's got secrets, Mr. Sutton. Dirty secrets. Just wait till the word gets out."

All the men at the table had risen, except of course Mr. Sutton, who couldn't. "Wayne," Bert snapped, his voice tight. "My decision today had nothing to do with Tyler. Look at you. You're drunk as a skunk, and this ain't the first time."

Mr. Sutton's face was dark with anger. In a low growl he addressed Wayne. "My son ain't got no secrets from his family. And you should know, I don't take kindly to anyone threatenin' my kin. So you just take that bottle and get your butt back to the bunkhouse. Sleep it off tonight, then pack your bags and git, you hear? I'll have a check for two week's pay drawn up, which is more than you deserve."

Wayne's mouth had fallen steadily open as Mr. Sutton spoke, his eyes at first widening with confusion and then narrowing with dawning comprehension. "You firin' me?" he spluttered. "You can't do that. I know stuff about your boy that'll get him tarred and feathered in this county—"

"You better not be threatenin' my family, Hurley," Mr. Sutton barked, half-rising from his seat, despite the cast. Tyler started toward Wayne, his fists clenched. Clint and Bert moved quickly in tandem, as if they'd previously rehearsed their movements, reaching Wayne before Tyler did.

They each took an arm, their hold none too gentle. Together they dragged Wayne across the floor, not stopping until they were outside. Tyler was right on their heels.

Wayne tried to wrench himself from their grasp, but drunk as he was and the fact it was two against one, left him beat. "Damn it, Bert," he said, his voice rising in a whine. "Y'all can't fire me. I know stuff."

Bert let go of Wayne's arm and moved up close, his face nearly touching Wayne's. Clint loosened his grip on Wayne's other arm, but didn't let go. "I'll tell you what you know, Wayne," Bert said in a low voice that had steel just beneath it. "You know this family doesn't tolerate bullies and assholes. You know this family's been around these parts for a lotta generations, and if a drunken bastard like you starts makin' trouble for the Suttons, well, there's gonna be trouble in return."

Wayne jerked from Clint's grip and staggered back, looking from man to man. It was clear from his angry, confused expression that he hadn't quite taken in what had just happened to him. "You can't fire me," he said again, the protest weaker this time. He lifted the bottle and tipped it to his mouth. Amber liquid trickled down his chin and Clint felt almost sorry him.

"Go on back to the bunkhouse," Tyler said. "You heard my father. Don't make it worse on yourself. You're no longer welcome here."

Wayne's jaw worked, but no sound issued from his lips. He threw the empty whiskey bottle to the dirt, scowled and then shrugged. Finally he found his voice. "Well, guess what, Sutton? You can't fire me, 'cause I quit." He glared from one to the other, as if he'd somehow scored a great victory. Then he staggered off in the general direction of the bunkhouse.

"I better follow him and make sure he gets where he's goin'," Bert said.

"I'll do it," Tyler said.

"I'll go with you," Clint added, moving closer to him.

Bert nodded. "Okay, then, but y'all hurry back. Me and Sarah have got some news, and I don't want that son of bitch to ruin it for us."

Tyler and Clint followed at a distance of a few yards as Wayne weaved and staggered toward the bunkhouse. It was unclear if he'd even remember what had just transpired when he woke the next morning. He entered the building, slamming the door behind him. They waited a few moments, and Clint said, "I don't think he's comin' out again. Probably passed out before he even got to his bunk."

"Let's hope so," Tyler said, a scowl on his face.

They walked back toward the house in silence. Just before going inside, Clint reached for Tyler, gripping his shoulder. He looked searchingly into Tyler's face. "You gonna be okay?"

Tyler slowly smiled. "Yeah. I think I'm gonna be just fine. Better than fine." Clint smiled back, wishing he could kiss Tyler then and there. But that would have to wait till later.

Once inside, they took their seats again at the table. Mrs. Sutton began to apologize to Clint for the disruption, but Clint assured her everything was fine. Beneath the table, he put his hand on Tyler's thigh and offered a comforting squeeze. Tyler placed his hand over Clint's and squeezed back.

Bert got everyone's attention by tapping his glass. "Ahem," he said. "Before that skunk busted in here, I had my speech all planned. I'm not gonna let him ruin it for us. Right baby?" He looked toward Sarah, who smiled back encouragingly at him and nodded. Bert again faced the table, looking toward his mother-in-law. "Me and Sarah got somethin' to announce." When all eyes had turned to him, he flushed and looked toward his wife with a comically beseeching expression. "Why don't you tell 'em?"

Sarah smiled, the same shy sweet smile Clint had seen on Tyler's face. "Well, we've been waitin' just to make sure, but the doctor said it's okay to say now."

"Oh, honey," Mrs. Sutton breathed, a hand fluttering to her mouth, her eyes filling with tears.

"That's right, Mama. We're gonna have us a baby."

Amidst the laughter and congratulations, Mr. Sutton's loud voice boomed out. "Well, there, you see? We find out Tyler ain't never gonna give us an heir, but at least Sarah here has come through. The Lord giveth and the Lord taketh away."

"Oh, shut up, Dad," Sarah and Tyler cried in unison, but Clint was glad to see they were both laughing.

~*~

Tyler and Clint were lying together in his loft. It was late and Tyler was bone weary, not so much because of the long day, but because of the emotional impact of facing not only Wayne Hurley, but his closely held secrets with his family.

Clint held him in his arms, somehow sensing now wasn't the time to make love, though Tyler knew if Clint so much as kissed him, he'd ignite the fire that always burned just below the surface when he was with his dominant lover.

But Clint just held him, stroking his cheek tenderly as he listened to Tyler talk. Tyler had warmed to Clint's approval as he'd related the details of the confrontation with Wayne and the conversation with his dad.

"I was so proud of you at supper, Clint," Tyler said. "The way you stood up to my dad. I mean, you were totally respectful, but you didn't let him pull any punches. It was great."

He could feel Clint smiling in the darkness. "I've met a lot of men like your dad, Tyler. My own father bein' one of 'em. It's not that they're bad men—they're just ignorant. They need educatin'." Tyler snuggled against Clint, feeling safe and happy.

Clint continued. "I'd say your dad really stepped up tonight, standin' up to Wayne the way he did, refusin' to even listen to that bastard's hateful words. The timin' worked out well, too. You did good, talkin' to your dad right away this afternoon, and bein' honest. It's best just to be yourself and let folks realize the person they knew all along is still that same person, even if he does prefer someone built the same as him as a bed partner." He reached for Tyler's cock, chuckling as he gave it a playful squeeze.

Tyler laughed, his cock swelling at Clint's touch. They moved together, kissing and touching each other for a long while, before the words still pressing in Tyler's mind made him speak.

"Clint, it's great having you here with me. But what happens next? I know you said you have the week off, but what then? You've got your job back in Ransom Canyon, and I'm needed here. What happens to us?"

"It's only two and a half hours from here to my place, Ty. It ain't like we live in different countries. If we want to be together, we'll find a way. I know you're needed now to pick up the slack, but they got along fine without you when you left, and from some of the things you've said since I've known you, your heart ain't necessarily set on spendin' the rest of your life at the Double S Ranch."

"It's true. I didn't only go to get away from Wayne. I think I needed to go in order to finally grow up."

"It's understandable," Clint agreed. "And that don't mean you have to stay here now, either, if you decide it's not right. You got options, Ty, plenty of 'em. And the same goes for me. I've put in my time at the bull ranch, but I'm not ever goin' to be more than foreman there. There's a whole passel of sons in line to actually run the place. But I've been savin' my money for a long time. I had a few bulls of my own over the years I was able to sell for a pretty good price. I've been bidin' my time, thinkin' 'bout maybe strikin' out on my own one of these years, if the mood ever took me."

He pulled Tyler closer, adding. "I'd need me a good partner to get things goin' and make a real go of it. Someone who knows the ins and outs of runnin' a ranch."

"You mean like Jonas?" Tyler held his breath. After all, as much as they seemed to be in love, Clint had known Jonas for years. He didn't want to fool himself on any score, or make assumptions that would only cause him pain.

"No, not like Jonas, you dope." Clint laughed and ruffled Tyler's hair. "Jonas is happy as a pig in shit just where he is. He's got no ambitions in that regard, trust me. I was thinking of *you*. If you were interested, of course."

They were both quiet and Tyler struggled to absorb the import of what Clint had just proposed. "I'm not talkin' tomorrow, or even necessarily this year," Clint continued in a quiet voice. "It's just somethin' I've been thinkin' about. Plannin' for, should the timin' be right. All I'm sayin' is, there's possibilities. Don't hem yourself in. There's a whole world out there."

Clint reached for Tyler, finding his lips with his own. They kissed a long while, tongues exploring as their hands roamed eagerly over each other's naked body. When they eventually fell back beside each other, Clint said, "We got somethin' special, Ty, you and me. I been lookin' all my life for you, only I didn't know it till I found you. Whatever else happens, we got each other."

He reached for Tyler's wrists, catching them in one hand and lifting Tyler's arms over his head on the bed. A shudder of lust moved its way through him at the dominant gesture. Clint leaned up over him, kissing him on the mouth, no longer a gentle caress, but a claiming with lips and tongue that left Tyler gasping when he finally let him go.

"You packed your silver-handled cock whip like I told you?" Clint rasped in his sexy voice.

Tyler gulped, his cock now hard as steel. "Yes, Sir," he whispered and then, impulsively, "I love you, Clint."

"I love you, too, Ty. With all my heart."

Epilogue

"Here we go, hot off the grill." Clint came to the long picnic table where Tyler's family sat, a platter piled high with smoked ribs and sausage.

"Set that plate right here in front of me, son," Tom Sutton boomed. "Them ribs look mighty fine."

"Leave a little for the rest of us," Sarah laughed, as Tom forked a full rack of ribs onto his plate.

Tyler appeared from the kitchen door, a large platter of steaming corn on the cob in one hand, a basket of biscuits in the other. Linda was moving around the table, filling everyone's glass with lemonade. Baby Emma, already nearly a year old, reached out a chubby fist from her perch on her daddy's lap to grab a slice of watermelon.

They were celebrating the successful opening of the DS Bull Ranch, Clint and Tyler's fledgling enterprise. Folks assumed the name was a combination of their last name initials—Darrow and Sutton. And while it could stand for that, it was also a secret nod to their D/s lifestyle, a fact that tickled Clint when he thought about it.

They'd bought an old, defunct ranch about an hour from the Sutton place. It had once been a working ranch, but had been abandoned due to bankruptcy, and had sat fallow for several years. They'd gotten it cheap, but there had been plenty of work to do just to get it to zero. With Clint's savings and Tyler's smarts, they'd procured the funding to buy the twenty-acre property, along with new fencing, a feed bunk, a hayrack, and a new water tank and pump.

The previous owners had apparently kept horses, or had planned to, because the state-of-the-art horse stable was barely used, and had taken only a little elbow grease to make it like new. The cow barn wasn't in nearly as good a shape, with a leaking roof and some foundation issues. They'd had a traditional barn raising party, attended by over a dozen local ranchers and their crews, and gotten the old barn refurbished and water-tight.

Joe Henderson, Clint's old boss, gave them two fine breeding cows as a startup gift, and Clint had purchased a very promising young bull who'd already sired several quality calves. They'd recently added six more cows to the herd. The Suttons had given them four horses, including Tyler's prized mare, Star. They'd fixed up the old farmhouse, which Sarah and Linda had helped to furnish and decorate, and the place really felt like home.

When they advertised for ranch hands, none other than Jonas Hall, seeing the ad in the local farm news, had shown up to apply. Clint hadn't realized how much he'd missed his old friend, so busy with his new life and new love. To his delight, Tyler had welcomed Jonas to the ranch, and he was living out back in the old bunkhouse. They used to invite Jonas over for the occasional BDSM play, but he had taken up with a fellow from a nearby farm, and that fellow was too possessive of Jonas to share. Jonas, also in love for the first time, and apparently in hog heaven, didn't mind a bit.

So far the three of them were managing the ranch, but just barely, with everyone working from dawn to dusk, seven days a week. They really needed a fourth hand, but didn't yet have the income to hire one.

But Clint wouldn't have traded his life for anything. Tyler and he had gone deeper into their D/s exploration, now that they had the time and privacy to fully embrace their lifestyle. Tyler now sported a small tattoo of ownership on his left hip—a coiled rope that symbolized the willing bonds he wore for his lover and Master. He also wore a gold chain around his neck that he'd never removed since Clint had given it to him. Only the two of them knew it was his slave collar. Clint was saving the gold nipple rings for Christmas.

Clint watched with satisfaction as his adopted family enjoyed the food and company on this pleasant spring evening. The baby was now covered in pink watermelon juice, and if Clint wasn't mistaken, there was a new bump under Sarah's dress, though they hadn't yet announced the big news.

Tom and Bert were talking about a horse they'd bought that was giving them trouble. Bert said, "We got us a bucker and a biter. She's a beauty, but she can't get acclimated to the saddle. You always had a gentlin' touch with the tough ones, Ty. Think you could find an afternoon one of these days to come take a look?"

"Sure, I'd be glad to," Tyler assented, glancing at Clint, who gave an affirmative nod. Family was family, and you always helped out family, no matter how busy you were.

They all turned to the sound of a car trundling up the gravel drive. "Wonder who that could be," Tyler said, getting to his feet.

"I'll go see," Clint said, putting a hand on Tyler's shoulder. "You enjoy your family."

He walked across the lawn toward the driveway, looking to see who sat behind the wheel. The man looked familiar, though he couldn't quite place him. He had dark hair, cut short, a strong nose and jaw. Then he turned his head, and Clint's heart twisted in his chest.

"Daniel," he breathed, stopping dead in his tracks.

Daniel opened the car door and climbed out of the car. When he saw Clint, his face split into a wide grin. He moved quickly around the car and in a moment they were in each other arms, both of them crying and laughing at the same time.

"Where the hell did you come from?" Clint said when they finally let go of each other. "Last I knew, you were in Munich, thinking about a move to Melbourne."

Daniel, having recently retired with a full pension from the military, had emailed Clint a while back, musing about what he wanted to do with the rest of his life, seeing as he was now forty-two, divorced and a civilian for the first time in over twenty years. Clint, done with keeping secrets, had finally decided to confide in his brother about his sexual orientation, and fill him in on what he'd been doing with his life. To his pleased surprise, Daniel had been nothing but supportive.

"Yeah, well, I figured it was about time I came back home, Clint. Back to Texas, back to the only family I have in the world. I had to see this new-fangled ranch of yours, and meet your fella." He grinned. "I wanted to surprise you, little brother. Did it work?"

"Shit, yeah, big brother. It sure enough did." He put his arm around Daniel, his heart surging with love and joy. "I hope you're planning on staying a spell. We have a guest bedroom all made up and ready. You'll be our first guest."

They walked back around to the side of the house, where Tyler and his family were eating, talking and laughing. "This here's my new family," Clint said to Daniel. "That handsome boy there is my one and only, Tyler Sutton."

The family looked up as the brothers approached. "Hey y'all," Clint said with a grin. "This here's my older brother, Daniel, come home at last."

Introductions were made all around, and Linda jumped up to make

Daniel a plate of food, whether he was hungry or not. Daniel took a seat on the bench beside Tom, who began to pepper him with questions about the military overseas.

Clint sat down beside Tyler, who took his hand under the table as their thighs touched. "What a fantastic surprise, huh?"

"It sure is," Clint agreed, looking Tyler over. "I'm wonderin' how he knew where we are. Any idea about that?"

"You mean, did you maybe leave your email open one day about a month ago and did I maybe happen to see the email from your brother, and did I maybe happen to notice his email address, and maybe happen to drop him a line that it sure would be nice if he came by for a visit? Something like that?"

Clint threw back his head and laughed. "I love you, Tyler Sutton," he said softly into Tyler's ear. "Did I ever tell you that?"

"You sure did, and they're the sweetest three words I ever heard."

Wild Stallion

The press of skin on skin, fingers entwined in silky mane

The ripple of sinew and muscle

Stallion heart gallops

A restless mouth seeking a bit

Powerful grace yearning for a rein

Longing for the binds to gentle its raging spirit

Desire rises like a spark from the campfire

Spitting its light beneath the inky black of a West Texas night

The cowboy tips his hat over his eyes

And dreams

Cowboy poet – Clint Darrow

Check out Book 3 of the Serving his Masters M/M BDSM Series!

Texas Surrender

If you climb into the saddle, you better be ready to ride...

JD Reed has the perfect life. Until he's fired from a great job in the morning and finds his sub boy in bed with another guy in the afternoon. So when he's told his family needs him back in Texas, he leaves New York without a second glance. He plans to help out at the ranch while his bereaved aunt figures out what's next. He didn't count on the brooding, tattooed ranch foreman who keeps stealing into his every waking thought...

Avery Dalton's hard life left him with few options until he found his place at Circle R Ranch. When his boss dies, he loses the closest thing to family he has left. When JD shows up, Avery is drawn to him like a horse to sweet grass, but he'll never trust the city boy. Though JD is clearly interested, Avery ignores his overtures—or at least he tries to.

Seducing the taciturn cowboy wasn't JD's plan, but the submissive nature hidden beneath the tough guy exterior calls to his dominant side. In a battle of wills that turns physical, the sexual tension seething just below the surface explodes like a Texas tornado, sweeping them both off their feet. But when the ranch is put up for sale, it all might end as quick as an eight-second rodeo ride. The boys can stay on the fence, or saddle up and take the reins.

Chapter 1

"I think Macy's gonna foal today or tomorrow. She's restless as hell. You got the fresh bedding ready for her, Avery?" Charlie called from outside. Before Avery could answer, Charlie let out a loud groan and then cried weakly, "Oh...dear god..."

Alarmed, Avery dropped the saddle he'd been oiling and ran out of the tack room. Charlie was standing by the paddock fence, a currycomb in his hand. But instead of grooming Kassie, he was clutching her mane and sagging against her, his face gray as wet ash.

"Charlie, what is it? What's the matter?" Avery hurried over to his boss, prying his clenched fingers from the agitated horse and gently helping the older man to sit down on the ground, not too close to the horse. Kassie snorted and flared her nostrils, tossing her mane and pulling against the rope.

Avery didn't have time to calm the mare, focused instead on Charlie. He lifted the hat from Charlie's head and pulled a rag from his back pocket to wipe at the sweat beading on Charlie's brow. He reached for the phone Charlie kept clipped to his belt and punched in 9-1-1.

Turning away so as not to alarm Charlie, he spoke in a low voice into the phone. "This is Avery Dalton over at the Circle R Ranch off County Road 38. I think Charlie Reed is havin' a heart attack. Send an ambulance, quick!"

Charlie was sweating profusely now, his hand clutching at his shirt, his breath coming in shallow, rapid gasps. Trying to keep the panic from his voice, Avery urged, "Just hang on, Charlie. Take it easy. Help is comin'."

He ran back into the tack room and grabbed a saddle blanket. Hurrying back to Charlie, he spread the blanket on the ground and helped the slumping man ease his head down onto it.

"It's okay. Just try to relax. The ambulance is on the way."

Charlie's eyes were glazed and unfocused, his breath slowing. *Don't die, don't die, oh god, please don't die.* Avery knew the mechanics of CPR, but it had been several years since he'd taken the training course.

"Hurry, hurry, god damn it," he muttered under his breath. He stood uncertainly, trying to decide if he could haul Charlie out to the truck and get him into town faster than waiting for the paramedics to arrive.

Kassie snorted and pawed the ground, whinnying softly. At the same time, Charlie's eyes rolled back and his mouth fell slack. "No," Avery cried urgently. "*No.*"

He could hear the ambulance siren as he knelt over the unconscious man and jerked open his denim work shirt, the armpits and front of which were soaked with sweat. He placed the palm of his hand flat on Charlie's chest and pressed in a pumping motion, trying desperately to stay calm.

Charlie didn't move. With trembling hands, Avery tilted Charlie's head back and lifted his chin. Pinching Charlie's nostrils shut, he took a deep breath and leaned over, sealing Charlie's mouth with his. He pushed breath into Charlie's lungs, feverishly praying that it wasn't too late.

~*~

JD was just tying his apron into place when he was approached by the chief chef of the Manhattan restaurant where they both worked. JD could tell by the frown on his face that something was wrong. When his boss told him to follow him into his office, he was sure of it.

Once seated, the older man launched in without preamble. "I'm sorry, JD, but we're going to have to let you go. Effective immediately."

"Excuse me?" Phillip could *not* be firing him. He must have heard wrong.

Phillip smiled sadly and shook his head. "You've done a great job as my sous-chef. It isn't about you at all. We just can't afford an extra chef right now." He stroked his jowls, as if trying to come up with the right way to say what he had to say.

"It's Andre," he said at last. "He wants this kept confidential—you know how the vultures will leap on any bad news and use it against us. But between you and me, Andre's bitten off more than he can chew with this new restaurant. The rent is eating him alive and the taxes are even worse. Until we get ourselves on better footing, we're cutting back everything we can.

"Who knows? Maybe in a few months? A year at most? We would want you back, definitely. But for now..." Phillip shrugged helplessly, holding up his palms in surrender.

Surely Phillip knew in this economy nobody was hiring sous-chefs, even ones trained at Le Cordon Bleu. JD would be lucky to get a job as a short-order cook at some diner in Queens.

He'd been hired eight months before at the French restaurant, which had just opened to rave reviews by some of the toughest food critics in the city. In a flurry of excitement, they'd quickly staffed up, but as often happened in the big city, diners were fickle, always eager to try something new.

JD was only one step below Phillip Stark, the chef de cuisine, and tasked with overseeing the preparation of his culinary masterpieces. After years of training and working for peanuts, he had finally made it—or so he'd thought.

Phillip pulled an envelope from beneath his apron and handed it to JD. "Your last paycheck, plus two weeks extra." JD stared with disbelief at the envelope, half-expecting it to crumble between his fingers, falling like stale bread crumbs to the floor. The years of struggle, of barely making it, holed up in some shit apartment, working his ass off to pay his way through Le Cordon Bleu had come to this.

He'd traded in the wide, open skies of the East Texas prairie for the cold, gray city in winter, and the muggy heat of a New York summer encased in concrete and glass. He'd put up with the rampant snobbery and condescension because he didn't come from the right background or speak with the right accent. He'd endured jibes about his Texas twang and his cowboy boots, and if the truth be known, felt more comfortable sharing a cigarette with the dish washers and bus boys in the back alley of the restaurant than debating which wine went with caramelized salmon with cherry mango salsa.

"I'm sorry," Phillip said again. "I'll give you the best references, I promise. You're young. You'll bounce back."

Young—yeah, right. And youth didn't pay the fucking bills. He was thirty-two, now unemployed, living in a one-room apartment he shared with roaches and rats. He had savings but they were sacrosanct—never to be touched until "someday" when he opened his own restaurant.

That prospect was receding even farther now in his dreams. JD walked along the crowded streets toward the subway, his mood growing ever darker as he pondered his souring fate. Instead of getting off at his stop, he kept going.

At least he had Tommy.

He'd stop and see his sub boy. Tommy worked from his home and with any luck he'd be there, clacking away at his computer. Tommy was a hardcore masochist. JD had pressed his sensual envelope as far as he dared, and had yet to find Tommy's limits.

They'd been lovers for the past few months. While JD enjoyed their BDSM play, something held him back from taking it to the next level. Their connection was intense, but remained primarily sexual. If JD took ownership of a sub, he wanted it to be for keeps. It had to mean something, something more than just hot sex and kinky games.

JD had a key to Tommy's apartment so when he came over to play, Tommy could be waiting, kneeling and naked on the floor, his leather wrists cuffs clipped together in front of him, ball gag in place. JD's cock hardened at that image as he walked down the stairs to Tommy's basement apartment.

He knocked lightly and waited, not wanting to just barge in unannounced. He knew, though, how absorbed Tommy could get when working and so after a minute he slipped the key into the lock and opened the door.

Tommy wasn't at his computer desk. JD opened his mouth to announce his arrival, but was stopped by a sound he knew well coming from the bedroom. It was the slap of leather against skin, accompanied by muffled groans.

Moving toward the bedroom door, JD pushed it open and stood, transfixed by what he saw. *His* boy, his personal sub boy who had told him over and over he was the only one, indeed had begged JD to collar him as proof of their exclusive relationship, stood naked, fingers laced behind his neck, a bright red ball gag stuffed into his mouth, a matching red blindfold over his eyes.

Clover clamps were attached to his nipples, a length of rope added to the chain and looped around Tommy' balls, which were purple from the strain. A man JD didn't recognize was standing fully clothed just behind Tommy, a heavy black leather flogger in his hand.

Once the shock of the moment released him, JD demanded, "Who the fuck're you?"

The man looked up and Tommy startled and jerked, gurgling against his ball gag. The man pulled the blindfold from Tommy's eyes. "You know this dude?" Tommy nodded, his eyes on JD, his expression pleading.

"Take the gag off him. Now," JD ordered and the mystery man obeyed.

Drool still sliding down his chin, Tommy blurted, "Oh, JD! I can explain! I'm so sorry. You aren't supposed to be here now. This was just a one-time thing, I swear."

The other guy was scowling. "What the fuck?" he interrupted. "Does this guy own you? You said you were free. What the hell?" Turning toward JD, the man opened his hands and held them out in supplication. "Sorry, man. I picked him up at Gertie's. He said he was looking for a real man. I didn't know he was your boy."

"He's not mine," JD replied with a calm he didn't feel. "In fact, he's all yours. Take him."

JD cut off Tommy's protests with a shake of his head. "I don't share, Tommy. I thought you knew that." Removing the key from his keychain, he tossed it onto the bed. Ignoring Tommy's pleas for him to wait, he walked back out into the August heat.

What could possibly happen to make the day any worse?

His cell phone began to ring. Without even looking to see who it was, JD answered with a surly growl. "Yeah."

"JD? It's Mom. I have real bad news about Uncle Charlie, baby."

~*~

So, that's the famous chef, Avery thought.

JD Reed was surrounded by his family. Charlie's brother had his arm around LuAnn, who was sniffling into a white lace handkerchief. That morning at the funeral was the first chance Avery had to lay eyes on JD, and he found he couldn't stop staring at him. When Charlie and LuAnn had talked about their nephew, the chef, Avery had envisioned someone short and fat, wearing a big white hat, like the guy on the can of ravioli.

But JD was broad-shouldered with thick blond hair and brown eyes the color of a sorrel chestnut mare. Despite the fact they were standing at a graveside, Avery, his head lowered, gazed at JD Reed from beneath his lashes, imagining that tall lean body without the covering of his fancy black suit. He shifted the Stetson he held in his hands to cover the press of his rising cock against his fly.

Avery didn't announce his sexual orientation, but he didn't try to hide it either. Charlie had treated him with a "don't ask, don't tell" kind of attitude, while LuAnn was pretty much oblivious.

Sometimes he daydreamed about having an actual partner—someone to come home to, someone to share his life with, but mostly he was content. When he got too lonesome, he'd make the eighty mile drive over to Dallas and find a guy to spend the night with. It wasn't an ideal arrangement, but it had worked out okay so far.

The casket was lowered, the dirt shoveled and amens murmured. As Avery watched, a wave of nearly paralyzing sadness washed over him. Charlie was gone. He wouldn't be coming back from a horse show in a few days. He wouldn't be there the next morning, already at work, no matter how early Avery got there. Never again would Avery hear his gruff bark of a laugh, or watch him calm a skittish horse, or feel the hard pat on his shoulder when he told Avery he'd done good.

What would happen now, now that Charlie was gone? He'd been the first person to treat Avery like he mattered. He was the first person to really trust Avery, despite knowing about his troubled past. He never judged Avery by his education or lack of it, or the fact he wasn't hooked up with "a nice girl by now", his mother's constant lament before she died. He recognized Avery shared his love of horses, and was willing to work hard, and that, for Charlie Reed, had been enough.

Avery blinked away tears as the dirt covered the casket, and turned away. LuAnn and her family piled into their cars to head back to the house. Avery walked back toward his old pickup truck and followed the procession.

He turned back, tipping his hat one last time to Charlie Reed.

At the house, neighbors and family swarmed, carrying plates piled high with food and talking in the hushed, muted tones saved for events like these. Casserole dishes and platters covered every available surface and the press of people around him seemed to be sucking all the oxygen out of the place.

"I better tend to the horses," Avery said, when he finally managed to get close enough to LuAnn to speak to her. "See how Macy and the colt are getting on." He vastly preferred the company of horses to people, and to top it off, he felt like he was going to jump out of his skin, which was itching against the cheap polyester of his Sunday suit.

LuAnn, distracted by the hovering crowd of women patting her and clucking sympathetically, nodded and waved vaguely toward him. The nephew, who stood near his aunt holding a bottle of beer, glanced toward Avery. Their eyes met and Avery felt a strange clench in his gut. The guy gave a barely perceptible nod, his mouth curving in the barest hint of a smile.

A kind of recognition passed between them, a knowledge that needed no words. Avery knew as those brown eyes raked his body like he owned him, that the nephew was receiving the same telepathic message.

He's gay.

It took a sheer act of will to break the contact between them, but somehow Avery managed to turn away. Who cared if the guy was gay? He was just passing through, a city boy with soft hands who would never look twice at the hired hand. A day or two of comforting the aunt and scoping out his uncle's will and the guy would be long gone. Meanwhile, Avery had a horse ranch to run, and no one to help him do it.

He walked down the long path that led from the main house toward the stables, pulling off the confining suit jacket and tie as he went. He'd just check on Macy before riding the tractor over to his cabin, located at the southern edge of the hundred acre ranch, secluded behind a copse of tall pines.

The ranch offered breeding and stud service, plus boarding. Two men could manage the average twelve to fifteen or so horses usually in the stable, but it was definitely too much work for one to handle alone. Avery hoped LuAnn didn't drag her heels on getting him help.

He unbuttoned his shirt and pulled it off as he entered the stable, which was cool in comparison to the hot August sun. "Hey, Macy, how you doin'? How's little Smokey?" If only Charlie could have hung on long enough to meet the new colt.

Four days prior, while life was ebbing from Charlie Reed, a new life was starting in the stall. Macy foaled a long-legged, wobbly colt that struggled to stand and plopped down again, only to try again and this time to succeed.

Now Smokey was nursing at the mare's teat. Macy looked over at the sound of Avery's voice and gave a toss of her head, as if to say, "My boy is doin' fine." Avery smiled, much relieved that the funeral service was over and he could get back to the tasks at hand. He would bury the sadness of losing Charlie by throwing himself into his work. The horses needed him.

They needed to hire a new hand before too long. George Harlan was looking for a permanent position. He was in his forties and knew his way around a ranch as well as anyone. Avery had always liked him, and felt bad when the ranch he'd been working at for so many years had shut down. It would feel good too, he couldn't deny it, to be the boss at last, the one in control.

He handed Macy a small apple he'd snatched from a fruit bowl in LuAnn's kitchen, patted her nose and turned to go.

"New colt?"

Avery was startled by the sound of a man's voice. He looked up to see the nephew standing at the door, his jacket slung over his shoulder, his tie gone and several buttons of his fancy striped shirt open at the throat.

"Yeah," Avery replied tersely, aware his mouth was suddenly dry.

The man entered the stable and looked around. "Boy, this place brings back memories. I spent some of the best summers of my life on this ranch."

Avery didn't reply. He kept his body averted, not certain if the erection that had again leaped to life in the guy's presence was showing. He wished he hadn't taken off his shirt.

The guy stepped closer, so close Avery could smell his cologne. He extended his hand. "I'm JD Reed. Charlie and LuAnn's nephew."

They shook, and Avery filed away the fact JD's hands weren't as soft as he'd expected, though nowhere near as tough and calloused as his own. "Avery Dalton."

"It's nice to meet you," JD said, without a trace of the New York accent Avery had been expecting. He looked Avery slowly up and down, and again a kind of thrill surged its way through Avery's gut. There was something powerful in JD's gaze. Something disconcerting that left

Avery feeling unsure of himself.

To cover his confusion, Avery drawled, "Like what you see?"

JD nodded slowly, a smile lifting one side of his mouth. "I sure do. Those are some tattoos. You into the pain?"

"Pardon?" Avery turned away, flustered by the question. *Was he into the pain?* What did that even mean?

He was very proud of his tattoos—the pure black Arabian horse rearing high on his right bicep and an Apache bow and arrow on his left. A stylized scorpion perched on the back of his neck, the tip of its curled stinger stained red. Out of sight on his hip coiled a diamond-backed rattlesnake, its silver tongue forking toward his groin.

JD's question was like a key turning in the lock of a door Avery had never dared acknowledge, much less open. Though he prided himself on his ability to take the inking needle like a man, he realized that until this moment he'd never consciously admitted there was more to it than that.

"You heard me. I asked if you get off on the pain. You know, like a sexual thing."

JD moved closer, so close Avery could smell the sweat beneath the cologne. There was a coiled tension in JD's demeanor, something raw and dangerous that both attracted and frightened Avery. His cock lengthened in his jeans, ignoring his mind's dictate to cut it out. He stepped back, nonplussed and embarrassed, the tips of his ears burning.

Hoping his swagger would fool the Yankee, he lifted the corner of his mouth in a sneer. "I have no idea what the hell you're talkin' about." For emphasis, he spat onto the clay floor. "Sorry I can't stay and chitchat, but I got a ranch to run. See ya' 'round."

He'd meant to walk away after that parting remark, but JD fixed him with a stare that kept him rooted to the spot. He had the disquieting feeling JD could see right into his head, and he didn't like it, not one bit. What the hell was going on? He needed to get away. He needed time to think.

Finally JD broke the spell. "Sure thing, Ave. We'll talk later."

Not if I can help it, we won't. Avery had to order his legs to walk, not run, aware of the man's eyes following him, his soft chuckle like a victory cry in the face of Avery's confused retreat.

Made in United States
North Haven, CT
05 May 2025